Also by Floyd Kemske

Human Resources
The Virtual Boss
Lifetime Employment

THE THIRD LION

A NOVEL ABOUT TALLEYRAND

BY FLOYD KEMSKE

CATBIRD PRESS
16 Windsor Road, North Haven, CT 06473
800-360-2391; catbird@pipeline.com

Our books are distributed by
Independent Publishers Group

First Edition

Library of Congress Cataloging-in-Publication Data

Kemske, Floyd, 1947-
The third lion : a novel about Talleyrand
/ by Floyd Kemske.
— 1st ed.
ISBN 0-945774-37-0 (alk. paper)
1. Talleyrand-Périgord, Charles Maurice de, prince de Bénévent,
1754-1838 — Fiction. I. Title
PS3561.E4226T48 1997
813'.54—dc21   97-14171 CIP

To
Gerry

I had to reach
deep for this one

Chronology of Talleyrand's Life and Times

1754 - Born in Paris and sent to live in the faubourg Saint-Jacques with his wet nurse

1758 - Elder brother dies; sent to live at Chalais with his grandmother

1760 - Sent to College d'Harcourt

1772 - Disinherited in favor of younger brother, Archambaud; sent to seminary at Saint-Sulpice

1774 - Coronation of Louis XVI; granted the abbey of Saint-Rémy and becomes financially independent

1778 - Meets Voltaire

1788 - Becomes Bishop of Autun

1789 - Elected to Estates-General as member of Second Estate on behalf of Autun; makes successful motion in National Assembly for Government to take over Church lands

1790 - Defeats abbé Siéyès in election to presidency of National Assembly

1791 - Resigns bishopric; ordains constitutional bishops; excommunicated from Catholic Church

1792 - Refuses to emigrate; secures commission from government to secure neutrality of England

1794 - Leaves for America when he learns he is about to be arrested under the Aliens Act

1796-1797 - Napoleon's Italian campaign

1797 - Returns from America and is appointed Foreign Minister by the Directoire; meets Catherine Grand; Napoleon's triumphal return to Paris; XYZ Affair, in which Talleyrand tries to extort money from American representatives

1798-1799 - Napoleon's Egyptian campaign

1799 - Napoleon's coup d'état on the 9th of November and declaration of himself as First Consul; Talleyrand remains Foreign Minister

1804 - Napoleon declares himself Emperor

1805 - Treaty of Pressburg

1806 - Made prince of Benevento

1807 - Meets with Tsar Alexander, leading to Treaty of Tilsit; resigns as Foreign Minister, but remains as Vice-Grand Elector of the Empire

1808 - King Charles of Spain abdicates in favor of his son Ferdinand, who in turn abdicates in favor of Napoleon's brother Joseph; Ferdinand and his brothers come to live at Valençay, and stay for six years; Talleyrand is still plotting with Tsar Alexander at Congress of Erfurt

1809 - Napoleon wins war in Spain

1814 - Allies enter Paris before Napoleon and the Senate and, egged on by Talleyrand, declare that Napoleon has forfeited his position as Emperor; Louis XVIII, Louis XVI's brother, becomes King and is induced by Talleyrand to sign a constitution; Talleyrand is made Foreign Minister and is a major figure at the Congress of Vienna, preserving France's borders

1816 - Dismissed as Foreign Minister due to a scandal

1817 - Appointed as Grand Chamberlain, a largely honorific post; not active in government for next thirteen years

1830 - Helps Louis Philippe take throne as constitutional monarch; appointed ambassador to Great Britain

1834 - Resigns ambassadorship and goes into retirement at the age of 80

1838 - Dies on the 15th of May

MAURICE

ONE

THERE ARE SO FEW things capable of amusing a man on the last day of his life. But it does amuse me that a sinner of my standing cannot be redeemed without paperwork.

All my life, people have been after me to sign things. My signature appears on every important treaty of this century, and now they want me to put it on a treaty with God.

Paperwork.

I flatter myself to think of it as a treaty; it is actually a recantation. It may guarantee a permanent cessation of hostilities between God and me, but in fact it merely describes three of my sins (the most trivial ones, to my way of thinking) and my regret for having committed them. I did not write this document. The one *I* wrote struck the local Church authorities as neither specific nor repentant enough to satisfy the Pope. So the monsignor and Father Dupanloup have collaborated in the preparation of this one, which they believe is dignified enough that I will not refuse signing and still abject enough that the Vatican will accept it.

But in negotiations, Father Dupanloup and the monsignor are children. I have negotiated with the Vatican, and I know what it will accept and what it will refuse. It will refuse to accept this recantation. It will demand one that is even more repentant, more apologetic, more groveling.

So I have delayed signing the document until this, my last day. My intent is that it will not reach the Pope until I am in the ground and incapable of revising it. Oh, the planning and preparation required for a deathbed conversion.

The dark rises momentarily, but when I look, the lamp flames are unwavering in their glass chimneys, and I understand it is not darkness gathering but my eyes failing.

There is a scratch at the door. Pauline has returned. She knows how much I cherish some of the older, gentler forms of life, and she has refused to adopt the bourgeois knocking and pounding with which the spirit of modernity approaches doors.

"Welcome," I say.

The brass handle turns, the door opens, and my precious darling enters. The lamplight makes her eyes glisten at the corners. I can see she has been weeping again. She approaches the bedside in a rustle of silk and linen and lays the back of her tender hand against my forehead. She will find nothing there. The faltering furnace of my body makes little heat these days. But I enjoy the touch of her skin on mine and the sign of her concern.

"Father Dupanloup is here, Uncle," she says.

Her mother and I told her some months ago who I am, but she never broke the habit of calling me "Uncle." I am glad for her sake. I will soon be far beyond the reach of scandal, but she has most of her life before her, and there are uncharitable elements who would delight in branding her the daughter of incest. It is not real incest, of course, since Pauline's mother, Dorothée, is only the wife of my nephew. But it is 1838, and the world still labors under the strange and ungainly moral code of our late Emperor, who prized family life above all other moral principles — the more so after he had put away his wife and married the Hapsburg princess on whom he thought he could get an heir.

"And what does Father Dupanloup want with me?" I tease.

"Please, Uncle." Her eyes shine brighter. I can see they are gathering more moisture. "He has come to see you sign your confession."

At eighteen, she is agreeably implacable. I wish I'd had her with me at Vienna. The force of her personality would have been useful in the Belgian question. And such a diplomat! She lets me think of this paper as a confession rather than a recantation. I can see she is troubled that I may not survive long enough to demean myself properly.

"Please tell him to wait," I say.

"Please, Uncle." Her lower lip trembles.

"Don't be frightened, child," I say. "I'm not." And I am delighted to discover that I have no overwhelming need to tell the truth even on this, my deathbed.

"Oh, Uncle." She sinks down beside the bed and lays her face against my dressing gown.

She remains in that position for a few moments, while her young body shakes briefly. She lifts her head and produces a handkerchief. My dressing gown is wet where her face was, and I find the dampness comforting.

"I wish I could remain longer with you and your mother," I say. "But I want no more than that. A man who has outlived his enemies can have no cause for regret."

"Uncle, you told me yourself that you regret your defiance of the Church."

I am trapped by my own remarks. How charming! She is truly her father's daughter. "Very well, then. Go to Father Dupanloup and tell him I will see him. But give me a moment."

She is smiling when she leaves me. I make myself smile in return. It is a skill I have perfected in many decades of government service and diplomacy. It is not easy to do now. I have sent her away because I have found it difficult to breathe.

I lie in this bed, and I suck the air, but my lungs do not respond. A roaring rises in my ears, and I wonder if this is the time. I wish I had not sent Pauline away.

And then she is beside me again, weeping.

"Oh, Uncle, Uncle."

She gestures to her confessor, Father Dupanloup, who is wearing his vestments and carrying a vessel of anointing oil. He steps forward eagerly, but then stops himself, shakes his head, and steps back.

Pauline looks stricken. She throws herself against my dressing gown again.

She fetches up against me like a blow to the chest. The rope around my throat has loosened, and I find myself able to make a wheezing gasp. The air, even in this closed-up room where I have been dying for months, is sweet in my throat.

"Thank you, my dear," I manage.

She looks alarmed, and her confessor looks disappointed.

"Oh, Uncle. We thought you were gone."

"There are doubtless others whom God wants to collect first," I say.

"Father Dupanloup would not even have been able to administer extreme unction. Once you have signed, he will be able to anoint you."

Father Dupanloup smiles serenely. He is a strapping young man whose whist playing is hampered by a tendency to show the contents of a hand in his face. His conversation is nearly as artless, but he means well and seems to care for the fate of my soul. And if he lacks

Pauline's unmitigated determination to get me into heaven, at least he applies as much effort to it as he does to the advancement of his career in the Church. It may well be the same thing.

The thought crosses my mind that I am a dying man and have scant time remaining. I should not have to put up with a priest at my bedside if I do not want one. But it is perhaps too late in my life to begin behaving rudely.

"Welcome, Father Dupanloup."

"Prince Talleyrand." Father Dupanloup approaches my bed. "I bring you my warmest regards and best wishes for your comfort."

One can enjoy a bit of dissimulation, even from such an awkward practitioner as Father Dupanloup. He has not come out of concern for my comfort. He has come to persuade me to sign the paper. I know how treaties are negotiated, and I know we will discuss many things before we come around to the welfare of my immortal soul. Father Dupanloup thinks I am the prize in this game. Perhaps I am the opposing player.

I distort my face into a smile again. "I cherish your regards, and I am grateful for your kindness."

"God protects us, Prince," he says. "We have but to ask."

Ah, he makes a strong opening move. He intends that I will now beg him to help me plead for God's protection, which will be vouchsafed me, of course, as soon as I sign the paper recanting my three sins. God apparently does not wish to admit those who have not first given over their dignity.

"Would you care to sit down, Father?"

Father Dupanloup sits in the chair in front of the bed.

"It is through confession and repentance," says Father Dupanloup, "that one is able to go to God as a child goes to his father — with fear perhaps, but always with faith

in his justice and his love." He glances toward the recantation on the nightstand.

I find myself wishing for a more accomplished player
in this match.

Two

ON A BRIGHT, snow-damp day, Maurice
and the other two children fled before Agathe's furious
housecleaning to chase larks in a field near their cottage.
Françoise and Jean-Marie did the chasing. Maurice's role
was to sit in the wet snow, the dampness soaking
through the seat of his tattered trousers, and shout
encouragement to the others. For all the good his cries
and squeals did, he might as well have been cheering the
birds as the other children.

Jean-Marie had dived into so many snow piles that he
was wet to his skin. The birds considered him very little
threat. He left his jerkin in a pile on the ground and
chased the birds in his shirtsleeves.

"I shall tell Mama you took your jerkin off," said
Françoise.

But Jean-Marie did not hear her. He dove toward
another bird. It flitted away as soon as his shadow
touched it, which was long before he arrived. Maurice
laughed to see Jean-Marie end up with handfuls of snow,
and he applauded.

He was still clapping when a shadow fell across him
and the warmth of the sun on his skin turned to chill.

Had he been a bird, he might have flitted away. He was,
however, not a bird. He looked up to the source of the
shadow and saw standing between him and the sun a
man. He could not make out any of the man's features,
but he was tall as a cathedral and straight as a pike.
There were other men in the background. Maurice was
only four and could not yet count, so he did not know how
many other men there were. More than one, but not a
crowd. They were all wearing uniforms.

Maurice looked around for Françoise and Jean-Marie
so that they all might leave together. But his companions
were already running away.

"Jean-Marie!" he called.

Jean-Marie, nearly to the road, looked back over his
shoulder, but did not break stride.

Maurice could not run. Alone in the shadow of the
cathedral-sized man, he stared at the wet grass in front of
him and shivered in the sudden cold.

For a moment there was no sound but that of the
man's cloak rolling in the breeze like a great flag.

"Are you the one they call Maurice?" he said.

"Yes."

"Come along then."

Maurice felt the sun on him again. He looked up and
saw the man's back, for he had turned and was walking
away, his cloak swirling behind him. The stranger meant
for Maurice to follow, as the other men were doing.

He felt he had no choice. He started after them on his
hands and knees, which was the only way he went anywhere.

The men were nearly out of the field and onto the
road when one of them, a younger man in a handsome
uniform, turned back to look. He saw that Maurice was
crawling, and he left the others to come back and stand
over the boy. Maurice was prepared for some sort of re-

buke, but the young man cast a smile full of sympathy and called out to the cathedral-sized man.

"Capitaine!"

The cathedral-sized man stopped and turned around. Now that he was no longer blocking the sun, Maurice could see his features. He had a strong nose and chin, and his face lacked the pockmarks the boy had seen on the faces of the other adults in his life. He wore a large, three-cornered hat of dark blue, from which the lower curls of a white wig protruded over his ears. He pushed aside the edge of his cloak, and his pale blue blouse sparkled with shining brass buttons.

Time stopped as he walked back toward Maurice. The boy wanted to crawl away or hide, but Capitaine wore an expression that suggested it was better to remain where he was.

"Can't you walk, boy?" said Capitaine.

But the sympathetic young man answered for Maurice.

"He appears to be lame, sir."

"Lame, you say?" The big man stepped forward. "Are you lame, boy?"

Maurice wondered why the man would ask such a question when the answer sat before him.

"Yes, Capitaine," he said.

"How did this happen?"

Maurice was four years old. For all he knew, he had been born lame. He said nothing.

The silence stretched on for a long time. Finally, Capitaine spoke again.

"A Périgord in rags, chasing larks with vermin. And now lame. Has no one sent for you before now? Do they even know you are lame?"

He gave Maurice no opportunity to say anything.

"My sister shall hear of this." Capitaine looked at the sympathetic young man. "Bring him."

He then turned and walked away.

The sympathetic young man bent and scooped Maurice up in his arms. "Come along, young comte."

There was affection in his voice, and Maurice was delighted with the nickname. The young man's manner put him at his ease, and he felt safe in his arms.

"Who are you?" said Maurice.

"Lieutenant Henri Lamoignon," he said. "I serve your uncle on the brigantine *Dragonet*."

Notwithstanding unfailing rebukes about it from Agathe, it was Maurice's habit to follow one question with another. He might have asked what it meant to be a lieutenant or what a brigantine was, but he seized on the part of the midshipman's answer that related most closely to him.

"Who is my uncle?"

Lieutenant Henri Lamoignon nodded his head toward the cathedral-sized man, who — now that Maurice sat at a more reasonable height — appeared to be merely man-sized, although extremely well dressed. "That man there, young comte. He is the captain of my ship, and he is also the bailli de Périgord."

"Why do you call me young comte?"

But the lieutenant did not answer, for they had arrived at the edge of the field, where a coach and four was standing in the muddy roadway. A driver sat on top of the coach at the front end, holding a whip and reins. There was a door in the side of the coach, and there was another seat on top of the coach at the back end. The bailli de Périgord turned to the lieutenant and Maurice, and motioned with his head toward the rear of the coach.

The lieutenant carried Maurice to the back end of the coach and effortlessly lifted him up to the seat. Maurice slid himself onto the hard wooden surface and sat above the road at a dizzying height. Then the lieutenant grasped the handholds and hoisted himself up to sit beside him.

The coach listed on its springs as the bailli de Périgord climbed in the side door, and only righted itself once the last of the uniformed men had climbed in after him. Maurice thought the bailli de Périgord kind in allowing Lieutenant Henri and him the seat of honor at the back of the coach. They had a commanding view of the countryside and the faubourg Saint-Jacques. The door clapped shut below them, and a muffled shout came from within.

"Drive!"

The coach surged forward, creaking and jingling.

It seemed to Maurice they moved with the speed of the wind. They overtook Françoise and Jean-Marie, who were running alongside the road, and Maurice delighted in their shocked expressions when he waved and shouted to them as if he were the one driving this magnificent conveyance. After they had become specks in the roadway behind, Maurice turned back to his new companion.

"Where are we going, Lieutenant Henri?" he said.

"I am a sailor," said the young man. "I rarely know the where. I go where your uncle tells me to go. He is my captain."

Maurice had never met anyone quite like the lieutenant. There was a sparkle in his eye and a smile on his face, at least when he was not addressing the bailli de Périgord. He was tall and strong, and he wore a most impressive uniform. And he spoke to Maurice as if the two of them shared a secret.

Maurice decided he wanted to be a sailor, too, although he hesitated at the idea of going where the bailli de Périgord might tell him to go. He was impressed with the bailli's kindness in letting him ride atop the coach, and it was clear the bailli had the respect of the lieutenant, but Maurice did not think he liked the man.

Their speed picked up even more. The coach wheels

and the horses' hooves threw off clots of mud, which spattered the coach and spotted the lieutenant's overcoat.
Maurice felt himself pelted with mud clots, but he paid
them no attention. He had been spattered with mud many
times before, and he knew it would not hurt him,
although it sometimes made Agathe impatient when he
brought it home on his clothes.

The breeze up in their moving aerie was strong
enough that Lieutenant Henri was obliged to chance the
mud clots and remove his hat, lest it blow away. His hair
was bound up in a ribbon at the back of his head. It was
clean and well-ordered, and it shone. Maurice reached up
to his own hair and felt a tangle of greasy curls. He found
a small twig there, which he tossed from the moving
coach.

The lieutenant laughed. "I wasn't much better yesterday," he said. "The first thing we do on reaching port is
get bathed and barbered." He looked at the brown spots
on his coat sleeve. "It appears I will have to do it again
today."

"Have you been on a journey?"

"We have just returned from a voyage to Africa," he
said. "We shall be putting out again within a few weeks,
but the captain wanted to see his nephew."

Maurice had never heard of Africa before, and he
would have asked about it, but he suddenly realized that
Françoise and Jean-Marie would arrive home without him.

"I hope Jean-Marie remembers to go back for his jerkin," he said. "She will be very angry if he goes home
without it." Jean-Marie's punishments, of which he'd had
many, were always harder when Maurice wasn't there to
plead his case with Agathe.

"Do you mean the wet nurse, young comte?"

"Why do you call me 'young comte'?"

"I believe that is what you are," said Henri.

Maurice had heard of comtes before, but he had never

entertained the notion he might be one. He had never
lived anywhere but in Agathe's penurious household. She
had never let him call her Mama, so he assumed he was
not her child, but he had no idea whose child he was, and
until now he'd had more important things to think about.

"Shall I be home in time for dinner?" said Maurice.

"I don't know," said Henri.

It was clear to Maurice that Henri had shared his entire supply of answers, and it would be of no use to ask
any more questions, so he settled himself in to enjoy the
ride.

As they left the faubourg, the buildings became more
imposing and more frequent. The coach's wheels bumped
onto a roadway paved with stone, and the sounds of
travel turned from a throaty creaking to a rasping buzz.
There was no more mud flying, and the horses slowed to
a walk.

The coach stopped in front of a grand house. A man
wearing a black jacket and knee pants came out of the
house and opened the coach door.

Maurice saw the bailli de Périgord alight.

The bailli turned and looked up at the lieutenant.
"Bring him," he said.

The lieutenant jumped down, then held his hands
aloft and encouraged Maurice to jump into his arms. The
jump was exciting, and Maurice thought this was truly
the finest day he had ever known.

The other men remained in the coach, and the lieutenant followed the bailli, who was shown by the jacketed
man into the house. They came into an entry hall large
enough to hold Agathe's cottage. The black-jacketed man
took the bailli's hat and cloak.

The bailli was an imposing figure in his powder blue
uniform with its brass buttons, fringed epaulets, and gold
braid. His wig was impressive as well. It was entirely

white and quite thick. There were three rows of large, round curls on either side of his head, covering his ears. A dashing black ribbon was wrapped around his right arm and hung down to his elbow. Unhatted and decloaked, he set off across the hallway with one hand on his sword, his heels clicking so rapidly on the marble floor that his black ribbon streamed behind him. Lieutenant Henri did not take the time to shed his coat, but fell in behind his captain. They walked the length of a long hallway, and they passed paintings of grand-looking people in serious poses.

The hallway was the largest indoor place Maurice had ever seen. At each of the many doors they passed, another black-jacketed man bowed in their direction.

They passed through several enormous and well-appointed rooms to get to the other side of the house, where finally they came upon a room filled with well-dressed women, all in black. They were sitting in various attitudes about the room, talking quietly among themselves, but the talking stopped as soon as the bailli entered. They all jumped to their feet and curtsied. It was by no means a military exercise, and each of them followed her own timing, so that the room was filled with randomly bobbing women. Maurice was captivated by two enormous white dogs asleep side by side against the opposite wall. One of them raised his head and looked at the bailli, but he put it down again and went back to sleep. The dogs appeared to be much more relaxed than the women.

On the wall above the dogs was a large painting. It was a portrait of a little boy, not much older than Maurice himself. He was seated, and a large sword in a scabbard lay across his lap. The scabbard was tied with ribbons and devices. The boy had one hand on it, and the other grasped an ornate medallion on a gold chain about his neck. Maurice thought he had never seen anyone look prouder. The picture's frame was draped with a black sash like the ones Maurice had seen on the statues at church, which Agathe had told him was part of Lent.

A man, the only one in the room besides Maurice's companions, stood before a set of double doors on the other side of the room. The doors were each carved with scenes of people and angels, similar to the wall paintings Maurice had seen in the little church he attended with his family in the faubourg Saint-Jacques, only much more realistic. The man in front of the doors was dressed in the same black jacket and knee pants as the man who had met the coach at the front door. He bowed deeply when the bailli approached him. They spoke briefly about someone called "the comtesse," and then the bowing man opened the door and they entered the next room.

The next room was a little church, and Maurice thought it marvelous that someone would build a church inside a building. It would certainly make it much more convenient for attending mass on a rainy day. At the same time as he was excited to see each new wonder of the day's adventure, he found himself hoping to be home in time for dinner. He imagined himself describing this amazing place to Agathe, Françoise, and Jean-Marie over the evening's porridge.

The little church was filled with candles, all alight and burning so brightly the room needed no other illumination. There were painted statues of holy figures and scenes of holiness on the ceiling. A handful of pews were filled with people, nearly all women and all dressed in black. The bailli de Périgord knelt briefly at the side of the first pew and made the sign of the cross, then rose and started up the aisle. Lieutenant Henri followed suit, after rearranging his left arm to carry the bulk of Maurice's weight.

"Hold tight with both hands," he whispered.

Maurice clutched tightly to Henri's neck and felt the

lieutenant's right arm vanish from beneath him as it appeared at his forehead to make the gesture. Maurice was barely able to make his own sign before the lieutenant was up again and hurrying down the aisle after the bailli.

At the end of the aisle, before the steps leading up to the altar, was a small table, and on the table an ornate casket. It was a short casket, and it was opened to reveal a boy dressed in a dark blue satin that shone with the light of the candles. Maurice had seen caskets before. People died every day in the faubourg Saint-Jacques. But he had never seen a child-sized one, and he was impressed. He hoped Henri would carry him near enough to the casket to get a closer look at it.

But the bailli rounded the last pew and stood before the group of women who sat there. Henri turned as well and stood behind the bailli, so that Maurice had a view of the entire small congregation, most of whom regarded him with interest. He smiled. Then his attention was taken by the woman the bailli was speaking to. She was the most remarkable woman Maurice had seen in his life.

She wore a black gown that contrasted sharply with her pale coloring. It covered her body from the floor up to the base of her neck. At the neck, the gown had a collar, and even this was of black lace. Her hair was drawn up on top of her head in an enormous white pile and covered with a gauzy black veil that came down to her chin.

She drew the veil up over her forehead to speak with the bailli. Her face held a smile, but her eyes appeared deep and wounded.

The bailli de Périgord spoke so loudly that people must have been able to hear him all over the little church.

"Sister," he said, "I have come to offer my condolences. It is never easy to suffer the death of a child, least of all the first-born son. I am deeply sorry for you."

The woman smiled, and Maurice thought he saw a glistening at the corner of one eye. "Thank you, brother. He is in God's hands now."

"To be sure," said the bailli. "And we are left to look after our earthbound obligations to our family and our sovereign."

"Indeed," said the woman.

"This is the other reason I have come," said the bailli. "You must meet your *new* eldest son." He turned to the lieutenant and gestured at the floor.

The lieutenant stooped and gently set Maurice on the stone floor, which was smooth and cold and shone with the candlelight. Maurice's dirty rags left dots of mud on the stones around him.

"Madame, I have the honor to present you the heir of the princes of Chalais, a princeling whose coat of arms is a shield of gules with three gold lions, passant and crowned in azure, bearing the motto 'Answer But To God.'"

Maurice had no understanding of the bailli's words, but he understood by the tone of them that the man was giving something to the woman.

The bailli left off his speech for a moment and looked from the woman down to Maurice on the floor. "Your Highness, Charles-Maurice de Talleyrand-Périgord, you may kiss your mother."

Maurice was astonished. Did he actually belong in this finery and sumptuousness? Was he meant to dress in these clean clothes, crawl these corridors, and sit on these luxurious chairs? Was this beautiful woman, this goddess in the black dress, truly his mother? He smiled and started to crawl the few paces toward her.

She looked down at the boy, and her expression changed from one of deep sadness to one of fear and shock. Her eyelids slowly covered her eyes, while her face assumed the color and texture of alabaster.

Maurice stopped where he was, two paces distant, for she seemed as if she might shatter at his touch. Then her eyelids rose again, and her eyes were clear and hard as English glass. She spoke so softly that Maurice had to strain to hear her.

"My God," she whispered. "He is lame? Take him away."

THREE

MAURICE DID NOT SPEND very much time with his new mother. The adults decided to send him to a place called Chalais, home of the duchesse de Mortemart.

At Chalais, a servant carried him into a great room, even larger than any he'd seen at his mother's house. There was blue sky with clouds overhead, and an angel sat atop one of the clouds staring at him.

Maurice almost laughed with the pleasure of it. That someone would paint the sky on a ceiling!

Some of the walls were covered with tapestries depicting orderly battles, but there was one wall that was altogether clear, except for an enormous red shield. The shield had three gold lions painted on it. Each of them wore a blue crown. Maurice thought this appropriate. Agathe had once told him the lion was the king of beasts.

There was almost no furniture. Chairs and tables had apparently been moved to the sides of the room to make way for a large crowd of shabbily dressed people who stood in a snaking line. The men among them twisted

their caps in their hands. The women carried babies or
held children by the hand. Except for an occasional baby's
wail, everyone was silent.

The servant carried him past the lines of poor people
to the other side of the room, where the line of poor people ended at an opening in a pair of velvet ropes. Behind
the ropes sat an old lady on a velvet armchair with a
small, black lacquered table beside her. Arranged on the
table were jars of unguents, bunches of herbs, and small
vials.

The items on the table looked interesting, but Maurice
could not take his eyes off the lady. She wore a silk dress
trimmed with lace. Her sleeves were covered with ribbons
and bows in green, yellow, orange, and white. There were
layers of ruffles at her wrists, and her bonnet was fastened on with a large black velvet ribbon tied in a bow
under her chin.

There was a peasant kneeling before her, and while
Maurice watched, she retrieved a vial from her table and
gave it to him.

"Put three drops of this in wine," she said, "and take
it with your supper each day until the vial is empty. If
you don't take the entire vial, the sickness will grow
worse. Do you understand?"

The man nodded.

She reached out and touched his forehead with three
fingers of her right hand.

"May God heal you; the duchesse touches you."

The man's body appeared to soften under her touch.
He sighed and leaned closer to her. She held her fingers
against him for some time and never did take them away,
as if she were perfectly content to spend the rest of her
life with her fingers on the grimy forehead of this suffering man.

But the man seemed to sense that there were others

to be served. He rose slowly, then walked backwards toward the opening in the velvet ropes. Maurice was watching him walk backwards when he heard the woman speak again.

"Charles-Maurice," she said.

He turned his head and saw she was addressing him.

"Do you know how to measure bandages?"

"No," he said.

She gestured to the servant, who set him in an empty chair at her right hand. She took a small roll of cloth from the lacquered table and handed it to him. "Then you will learn. You will be my chamberlain, and it is the duty of a chamberlain to measure the bandages. You must hold the bandage for me to cut it with these scissors." She brandished a shining pair of scissors. "It is important the bandages be the proper length. Do you understand?"

"Yes."

"You shall address me as 'Duchesse,'" she said. "And I shall address you from now on as 'Your Highness.' Attend to me now. We are relieving these good people of scrofula, the king's evil. It is one of our responsibilities, and you should learn how to do it."

The duchesse healed dozens of people that afternoon. To some she gave medicines, to some warnings. Some approached with oozing wounds bound by filthy rags. For these, she leaned toward Maurice and instructed him to measure a bandage the length of his arm. She would then cut the bandage and offer it to the person in trade for the filthy rag, which one of the servants then dropped into an earthen pot. No matter what she did for the sufferer, however, she always ended her advice with a three-fingered touch of her hand on the person's forehead, and her blessing: "May God heal you; the duchesse touches you."

It was strange and wonderful sitting in the comfortable chair and watching the radiant duchesse heal these people and accept their grateful admiration. He nearly burst with the joy of it.

Even so, his bones felt tired by the time the last sufferer backed from the duchesse's presence.

The duchesse turned to Maurice. "Your Highness is the best chamberlain I've ever had."

It was his first experience of accomplishment and his first experience (other than the distracted affection of Agathe) of love. He, in turn, loved the duchesse in a way he'd never loved anyone before.

She looked at his blouse and his trousers and then at the rope fastened around his waist. She turned to the servant who stood behind her chair. "Send word to the tailor tonight. We need him after matins tomorrow." She turned back to Maurice. "A chamberlain must look like a chamberlain."

"Shall I cut bandages every day, Duchesse?" he said.

"We do this but once each season," said the duchesse. "Some great houses no longer do it at all. Even the King is under the sway of advisors who think thaumaturgy superstition, and he rarely ministers to the sick. But our family is older than the King's, so we do as we have always done. If we can relieve suffering in our community, we do not concern ourselves with who might think us superstitious."

"Are we superstitious?"

"My fingers have no magic powers, Your Highness," said the duchesse. "That's one of the reasons I give them medicines. But a sufferer with hope is half cured; the blood circulates with vigor, strength returns to the nerves, sleep comes at night, and the body revives. Confidence is the best physician. We owe these people so much, and we are able to discharge a portion of the debt when we give them confidence."

The duchesse looked upward in thought. Then she

spoke softly to the angel on the ceiling. "The King is said to believe our way of life is destined to be engulfed."

The angel did not reply, and the duchesse turned her attention back to Maurice. "At Chalais, Your Highness will find life as sweet as anything humanity has known since we left Eden. God has seen fit to apportion this sweetness to only a few. Most of the world's people live in misery. We, who are fortunate enough to truly know the pleasure of living, should mitigate others' suffering when we can. And if we cannot see that as our Christian duty, we deserve to drown in the King's deluge."

The duchesse brightened then. "Your Highness looks healthy and strong, in spite of everything."

Before Maurice could point out to her that he was lame, she began giving orders to the servants and took notice of nothing but the task of getting the pharmacy back in order so it might resume its responsibilities as a ballroom.

🦁   🦁   🦁

Maurice awoke in the night. He was alone in the bed, and he wondered where Agathe, Françoise, and Jean-Marie were. But he was at Chalais, wasn't he? He wore a nightshirt with an embroidery on the breast, and he shared a bed with no one. He wondered if he would ever see his foster family again. He would miss Agathe and the spare meals the family ate in the cottage. He would even miss Jean-Marie, notwithstanding he was always unhappy and always poking people.

He lay on his back and stared at the dark ceiling. It was a beautifully decorated ceiling, although now it was lost in shadow and darkness. The bedclothes were smooth and soft, and he pushed himself from one side of the bed to the other, enjoying the feel of the linens against the nightshirt and the feel of the nightshirt against his skin.

It was a beautiful nightshirt, white and spotless. On the front, to one side, was a colorful crest of a design that looked very similar to the great red shield on the wall of the pharmacy. He was restless, and he pushed himself from under the covers and out of the bed. It was a long drop to the floor, and he had to lower himself until he was close to the floor and then plop onto the carpeting. There was no fire in the hearth below the ornate mantle, but the night was warm. Moonlight streamed in through the window, and he could make out some of the flowered design in the rug. There was a desk on the other side of the room, by the door, and he crawled over to it. Holding one of its carved legs, he raised himself up beside it. He sat in the chair, and he could feel the seat cushion on his bottom through the nightshirt. He rubbed the palms of his hands over the surface of the desk. He would write letters here, just as soon as he learned to write and made the acquaintance of some people who might read his letters.

The candle on the table was hardly used and stood quite tall. He must be wealthy to have a candle this tall. At Agathe's house, they had burned candles down to nothing, then scraped the wax from the holders and collected it to melt into new candles.

The moon was high, and even without a candle he could make out most of the features of the room. Dark tapestries hung against the walls. The canopy over his bed cast a shadow across the floor in the moonlight.

What better time to explore Chalais?

He slipped out of the chair and dropped to the floor, then crawled over the carpet to the door. There, he pulled himself up by the wainscotting and holding on to the doorhandle he turned it. He dropped to the floor again and crawled over the threshold into the hallway. He left the door open, as he intended to return before morning.

There were no windows in the hallway, and the corridor was much darker than his room had been. But there was light at the end. It wasn't the white light of the moon but the yellow light of a lamp, spilling into the hall through an open doorway. He crawled down the dark hall toward the light.

The carpeting was red where the light from the doorway made a circle before him. He crawled into the circle and stopped, rocked back to sit on his heels, and looked into the room. There was a woman seated in a chair against the wall. He recognized her as his grandmother's handmaid. Her head was tilted back, her mouth was open, and she was snoring softly. A modest fire crackled in the hearth.

In a larger chair sat the duchesse herself. She wore a richly embroidered dressing gown shot with shiny green and gold. A high collar encircled her neck, and spectacles sat on the bridge of her nose. She was reading silently from a book. Without looking up from the book, she whispered to him.

"Come in, Your Highness, but quietly. We don't want to awaken Madeleine."

He crawled past the sleeping Madeleine to his grandmother. She closed the book in her lap and nodded toward an ottoman. He climbed up on it and sat at her feet.

"Madeleine attends me all day," said the duchesse. "I would rather not tax her by compelling her to stay up with an old woman, but she feels her place is here with me, and I am not one to deny a person her place."

He rubbed the coat of arms on his nightshirt with his fingers. "Do you not sleep, Duchesse?"

She looked at him over her spectacles, then she took them from her nose with one hand, folded them up, and held them on her book. "Our needs change when we grow older," she said.

"I shall be glad when I am older." A yawn took hold

of Maurice, crushed his eyes shut, forced him to take a great breath, and then left his eyes watering. "I shall be glad when I do not need to sleep," he said. "It's very boring to sleep."

"Aha," said the duchesse, as if the boy's opinion about sleep was the most important thing she'd learned that day. She looked up at the ceiling as she so often did when she was thoughtful. "Your Highness will be forgiven his ignorance, but we do not yawn in conversation." She looked back down at him. She was smiling, and the rebuke settled on him as softly as the bedclothes he had left down the hall.

"I could not help it," he said.

"One day you will," she said. "Your Highness should also be aware that we do not confess our boredom in civilized society."

"Why not?"

"We do not confess our boredom for the same reason we do not confess our longings, our grief, our disappointments, or our infirmities. We create our character on the inside, but we wear it on the outside. It should be at least as presentable as our best clothing."

"Is there no one we can tell when we are sad?" Another yawn stole over him. He fought it desperately before it finally pressed his face into a little ball and pried his mouth open.

The duchesse appeared not to notice the yawn this time, but she looked toward the ceiling again and stared into the gloom above for some time before she spoke again.

"From time to time," she said at last, "people meet other people with whom they can share these deep feelings. And if you meet such a one, you will share your character with that person, and as a result you will feel a need to be with that person. And when you are with that person, you will feel you have no need of anyone else in the world."

"Shall I meet such a person?"

"It does not happen to everyone." She looked down from the ceiling and smiled at him. "Your mother and father are such a pair. I think it is a source of consolation to them at court, where life can be most difficult."

Maurice took careful note of any revelations about his mother and father, for he had a nagging fear they might send for him and take him away from Chalais. Another yawn attacked him. He beat it back, practicing to keep the fight from showing in his face.

"Shall I go to court?" he said.

"Your parents attend the dauphin," she said. "They are not given very much time for their own children." Her voice and especially her eyes were rueful.

And Maurice was still thinking about the sadness in her eyes when he realized he was in bed. He opened his eyes and saw red sunlight pouring through the windows. He wondered how he had gotten back to bed. Perhaps he had dreamed the visit with the duchesse. But he looked and saw the bedroom door was open, the way he had left it the night before. He sat up in bed. He looked down at the crest on the front. He loved this nightshirt. Perhaps the duchesse would let him wear it to play in.

He was still sitting in bed when a small man came in. He wore a black coat, and he sat on the bed beside Maurice. He said hello, then he began poking and prodding him. He was not unfriendly, but he grasped Maurice's clubfoot with hands as hard as garden tools and muttered to himself as he twisted the foot, first one way, then another. While he was twisting, the door opened and Maurice's grandmother, attended by a pair of female servants, came into the room.

"Please forgive the intrusion, Your Highness," she said. "It is best we two are together for this."

The man massaged the boy's foot deeply, so deeply that it hurt. Maurice wanted to cry out, but he knew it would unsettle his grandmother, so he breathed hard through his nose and tried to smile. Finally, the man left off torturing him and turned to the duchesse.

"Did the Duchesse say this was an injury?"

"Yes," said the duchesse. "Apparently, when he was an infant he fell from a chest of drawers at the home of his wet nurse."

"Was the injury attended to at that time?"

"No, the poor woman was too afraid to tell anyone. She seemed to think it might heal by itself. The parents have been busy at court since he was born. I only found out about it days ago."

The man turned back to Maurice. "Do you walk, Your Highness?"

"No."

The man grabbed his bad foot again in the way a cook might grab a joint before haggling over it with the butcher. "I'm not surprised. Several bones were dislocated in the injury. There was a fracture that has healed out of alignment, and the muscles on one side are useless."

"What can you do for him?" said the duchesse.

"If you send for a carpenter, I can explain what he should measure to carve a brace. We can get the comte up on two legs, but he's never going to ride or fence, I'm afraid."

The duchesse turned to one of her servants. "Fetch Jacques." She turned back to the man as her servant left. "The carpenter will be here presently. Is there nothing else to be done?"

"If I had seen him within days after the injury, I think I could have done fairly well by him, but this late. . . " His voice trailed off.

"What will the brace be like?" said the duchesse.

"It must be heavy," said the man. "It has to hold him up. He ought to be able to walk short distances, though." He grasped Maurice's foot again. "With a limp."

The small man withdrew, and the duchesse looked at the boy with sadness.

Maurice did not completely understand what was happening, but he could hardly bear to see the duchesse look so sad. Then the duchesse approached him and laid her hand on his forehead and smoothed back his curls. Her touch was soft and gentle, and he wished it would go on forever. But she pulled her hand back and touched his forehead with three fingers in the same way she had touched the hundreds of peasants the day before.

"Would that I could heal Your Highness with a touch." She slid her hand down his head and grasped his shoulder. "But God has chosen to test you for the courage and forbearance of the Périgords."

Her touch was soft, and it felt good, but it scared him that she should be so upset. Was it because he could not walk? He had never walked, but he had never found crawling to be troublesome.

"I know He will not find you wanting," she said.

Maurice looked up at her, and he understood that being unable to walk was a serious matter indeed. He began to feel a stinging behind his eyes that he knew was the first sign of tears. He bit his lip to keep himself quiet. It was no use. Her image began to break apart as tears smeared his vision. He wiped his eye with his hand. He felt small and weak.

"I would like to tell Your Highness a story," said the duchesse. "Has Your Highness taken note of the crest on his nightshirt?"

Maurice looked down at the crest. A tear fell on it, and he was ashamed.

"Lions," he managed.

"Indeed," said the duchesse. "Your Highness reminds me of the third lion."

Maurice looked up at her.

She pointed to the shield on his chest. "Do you see how this lion has a shorter foot?"

Maurice looked at where her finger was pointing at the lowermost lion on the shield. It did not really look to him like the lion had a shorter foot, but it was his experience that grownups often saw things that were invisible to children.

"This lion stands up straight like the others, and he marches as they do," she said, "despite the pain of walking on a short foot."

Maurice squinted at the embroidery. Perhaps that foot *was* shorter. "Is that why the other lions have sent him to the bottom?" he said.

The duchesse smiled. "I hadn't thought about that before, but I believe you are correct. Your Highness has a very good sense of relationships."

Maurice was proud for having pleased her, and he found himself able to smile.

"He does not need to be at the top of the shield to prove he is the noblest of lions," said the duchesse. "He has nobility in his heart, and that is enough."

Maurice thought about the lion suffering with his pain in silence and taking comfort in the nobility of his heart.

"This lion lives by a principle, Your Highness."

"What principle?" said Maurice.

"His principle is, 'I do not complain,'" said the duchesse.

It sounded to Maurice like a grand principle. Brave and strong and filled with the dignity of the Périgords, who answer only to God. He no longer felt he needed to cry.

"Let us go to breakfast, Your Highness. The servants

will come presently to dress you. I will meet you in the dining room."

"May I have jam?"

The duchesse reached over to tug the bell-pull beside the bed. The door opened almost immediately, and a young man in Périgord livery appeared.

"Make certain there is jam for the comte in the dining hall," said the duchesse.

Four

MAURICE FOUND there were great pleasures to be had in fulfilling his obligations to the household and to the family at Chalais. As chamberlain to the duchesse, he performed his duties scrupulously. He learned the names of her guests and studied their ancestries and attainments, that he might help in getting them seated properly in the sitting room or served with appropriate ceremony in the dining room. And, of course, he carefully measured the bandages during thaumaturgy, basing them always on the length of his arm, so that with each season they grew a little longer. By the time he was six, the duchesse even remarked that the bandages were reaching quite a respectable length.

At Chalais, Maurice felt he belonged. Even the servants of the château seemed to love him. At least they loved his family, and they gave him whatever respect and affection was due its newest member. They addressed him as "young master" or "young comte." And he behaved graciously toward them all, under the guidance of the duchesse, a guidance he sometimes earned most uncomfortably.

The duchesse thought it unbecoming for the heir of the Talleyrand-Périgords to crawl about the estate on his hands and knees, so she assigned to him a strapping servant named Auguste, whose duty it was to carry him everywhere he needed to go. Auguste brought his breakfast each morning and was inseparable from him for the remainder of the day, carrying him about, helping him with his leg-brace, attending to him during afternoon walking practice. Auguste left him only for sleep and during mealtimes, when he withdrew to the kitchen to take his food with the other servants.

At the advanced age of eighteen, Auguste was quiet and shy. He had no sense of humor Maurice could make out and may well have been the worst playmate in all of France. But because he talked every day with the other servants, he knew more about the Périgord family than any of the Périgords. He was able to tell the young comte about Maurice's parents, and how much responsibility they had for the well- being of the dauphin at court. He explained to Maurice how his parents were a legend at court and abroad for the strength and depth of their marriage and attachment to each other. And he told him about his younger brother, Archambaud, who lived with a wet nurse near Versailles.

"I would like to meet my younger brother," said Maurice.

"Soon he will be four," said Auguste. "Perhaps they will bring him then."

Maurice thought it best that he learn as much as he could about Chalais, so he would be prepared to show the estate to his younger brother when he arrived. Together, Maurice and Auguste explored the château. The servant carried the boy up staircases and down corridors.

Together, they looked out windows, examined tapestries, opened cupboards, and yanked bell-pulls to summon servants for no reason.

At first, Maurice told Auguste to stop at every door they came to.

"Where does this door lead, Auguste?"

"This is the music room," Auguste would say, or "This is the white room."

And if Maurice wanted to see it, they would go in and Auguste would carry the boy around the room to examine it, explaining the functions and histories of various objects and pieces of furniture as best he could, which was often not well, but better than nothing at all.

Maurice preferred to spend most of his time in the great hall.

The great hall was lined with Périgord portraits. Maurice was saving the task of counting them for a time when he had nothing else to do and was more confident of his numbers. Auguste explained to him that these were pictures of the comtes, back to nearly a thousand years ago.

Some wore battle gear, some were dressed in court finery. Some had beards, some were bare-faced. Some rode horses and some sat in chairs. Despite all their differences, however, they all stared out from the paintings with the same eyes. These eyes were large, set wide from each other, and slightly closed, as if they'd been used too much and needed rest. They were the same eyes Maurice saw whenever he looked in a mirror.

Auguste was able to give him the names of some of the comtes, but he did not know all of them, and he was no more able than Maurice himself to read the small plaques that were attached to each frame. Maurice hoped to tour the hall with the duchesse one day. As they looked at each portrait, she could tell him the name of the comte, and Maurice would commit the name to memory, just as he did those of the château's innumerable guests.

He stopped Auguste in front of one of the portraits. It showed a bearded man in mail, holding a helmet in the crook of his arm. There were other men in the background, although they looked indistinct, and the only thing one could say about them was that they were armed. Maurice did not know whom they intended to fight. Perhaps the English.

"Who is this, Auguste?"

"I know him only as the horned one," said Auguste.

"What are you talking about?"

"He has horns," said Auguste, "there, on top of his head."

But there was nothing on top of the man's head except his hair. Then Maurice saw what Auguste meant. Behind the comte stood a group of soldiers, and some of them were holding pikes. The comte's ears covered some of the men holding them, but behind his head there were two pikes sticking straight up in the air. To a dull person like Auguste, they could look like horns. The picture began to make Maurice uncomfortable.

"Let us see something else," he said.

And Auguste bore him away, down yet another corridor, where they passed one of the plainest-looking doorways Maurice had seen in all of Chalais. Its panels lacked any sort of carving, and the handle was not brass but blackened iron. It was no larger than the door behind the grand staircase that led down into the servants quarters.

"What is this room, Auguste?"

Auguste looked as if he were making a decision about what to tell him. When he finally decided, he spoke hesitantly.

"It has pictures," he said. "They say it is the entrance to the College d'Harcourt."

"Let us see the pictures," said Maurice.

Auguste shrugged and turned the door handle with his left hand.

"What is the College d'Harcourt?" said Maurice.

"I do not know," said Auguste.

The pictures were all much smaller and plainer than those in the great hall. Not one of them had a name plaque on it, and they depicted the saddest people Maurice had ever seen. Their expressions were not improved by the room's general gloominess, for the curtains over the windows admitted a pale sort of light, and the modest table in the center of the room had a layer of dust on it, as if no one had been in here for a long time. The people in the portraits were all men, and all were dressed as priests of various ranks. Two of them wore the vestments of bishops.

"Who are these men?" said Maurice. "Why are they in this dark little room?"

"I only know what the other servants say," said Auguste.

"Out with it, then, Auguste," said Maurice. "You must tell me."

"There is only one comte," said Auguste. "But he always has brothers. In servant families such as mine, we live with our brothers. In great families, such as the Périgords, the brothers of the comte are sent away."

"Sent away?"

"To the College d'Harcourt," said Auguste.

Maurice looked at the sad men in the portraits. He thought at first that the College d'Harcourt might be a place like Purgatory, which his grandmother's chaplain had described to him. But then, they were all priests, and why would anyone want to punish priests?

"I shall not send Archambaud to the College d'Harcourt when I am comte," said Maurice.

"It is the way of the world, Your Highness," said Auguste.

"I am not one to follow the way of the world," said Maurice. "Let us go to the carriage house. This place makes me cold."

Auguste was delighted to comply, for of all the places in the château he loved the carriage house best.

That night, before Maurice went to sleep, he got on his knees beside the bed and prayed the way Agathe had showed him when he was little.

"Lord, bless the Duchesse and watch over her. Bless all the people of this house, and please bring my brother Archambaud to Chalais so that I may take care of him."

He could think of nothing else he might say that would interest God, so he ended with an "Amen" and climbed up into the bed. He felt he had done his best, and he slept that night like a little boy, which is to say, very soundly.

The next morning, Maurice sat in bed and waited for Auguste to come and fasten the ties of his shirt collar. He had already donned his hose and kneepants, though, and he was hungry.

There was a scratch at the door.

"Enter," said Maurice.

The door opened, and Auguste walked in. He had no breakfast tray.

"Why, Auguste," said Maurice, "where is my breakfast?"

"You breakfast with the duchesse in the dining room today," he said.

Maurice felt warm inside. Breakfast with the duchesse! "Let us go then, straight away."

Auguste bent over him and tied the strings at his collar into a bow. He stood up and retrieved a jacket from the wardrobe and held it while the boy slid his arms into the sleeves. Then he bent over Maurice to pick him up, but Maurice was too happy and excited to do things the way they were supposed to be done.

"Wait, Auguste," he said. "Turn around. You can carry me on your back this morning."

Auguste straightened up and looked puzzled. His face contorted with his concentration as he wrestled with the decision.

"Hurry," said Maurice. "We mustn't keep the duchesse waiting."

Auguste always moved quickly when given an order. He turned around and squatted in front of the chair. Maurice grabbed his shoulders and wrapped his legs around the servant's waist.

Auguste stood.

"Now then," said Maurice, "when I kick with this leg" — he bumped Auguste's side with his good leg — "we turn in that direction." He bumped his other side with the lame leg. It hurt a little, but Maurice did not wince. Not in front of a servant. "And when I kick with this one, we turn in the other."

Auguste nodded, and they started toward the dining hall. They descended the grand staircase into the foyer, and Maurice thought riding was a much finer mode of travel than being carried. In the broad foyer, he decided to see how well Auguste had learned the commands, and he bumped him with his good leg. The servant stopped.

"You're supposed to go that way." Maurice pointed across his shoulder.

"The dining hall is this way," Auguste said slowly.

"But you must go where I tell you," said Maurice.

"The dining hall is this way," said Auguste.

"But I am the one who says *how* we go." He thumped Auguste's side with his leg again, a little harder this time.

Auguste shrugged and started off in the direction Maurice had pointed.

"When I squeeze you with my legs," the boy said, "you must stop." He squeezed with his legs.

Auguste stopped.

Maurice thumped his other side with his leg, and Auguste turned back in the direction of the dining hall. The remainder of the trip to the dining hall was quite satisfying. Maurice stopped Auguste, turned him about, and even invented a command to make him walk backward.

When they finally entered the dining hall, they found the duchesse seated at the end of an imposing table of dark, polished wood.

"Good morning, Duchesse." Maurice waved to his grandmother as if he were mounted on one of the handsome horses in the riding paddock out back.

The duchesse's brow furrowed, and for a moment Maurice wondered what he had done wrong. But then she smiled, and he knew everything was all right. He should have known better than to suspect the duchesse of temper. She never had temper. She pointed at the straight-backed chair cater-corner from her own. Auguste pulled the chair away from the table and turned it about. Then he squatted in front of it so Maurice could climb off and seat himself in it. The chair had a cushion on the seat, and it was much more comfortable than it looked. Auguste straightened up, then walked around in back of the chair, picked it up, and lifted it in close to the table.

"Thank you, Auguste," the duchesse said, as warmly as if he had deposited an oversized pearl before her.

Auguste nodded and left the room.

"I would not thank him, Duchesse," said Maurice. "He only does what he is supposed to do, and he's not very likable. Yesterday, while we were looking at the comtes, he told me one of them had horns."

"That would be Hélie I." The duchesse gestured to a

serving girl, who stood at a sideboard by the wall. "Bring His Highness bread and jam, milk, and pieces of dried apple."

The serving girl brought a plate and set it in front of Maurice. He thought it looked like the most sumptuous breakfast he had ever seen. Although the duchesse rarely ate, her presence always made meals more sumptuous.

"Thank you," said the duchesse. "You may go."

The serving girl curtsied and left. Maurice thought it was graceful the way his grandmother always thanked people, no matter how slight the service rendered. He picked up a piece of dried apple and took a bite. It was sweet and chewy.

"I am certain Your Highness is aware," said the duchesse, "that he is a scion of one of the noblest families in all of France."

Maurice nodded. One could not look at all those portraits in the great hall and believe otherwise.

"Eight centuries ago, Hélie I, your illustrious ances-tor, gouged out the eyes of the Bishop of Limoges."

In his mind, Maurice saw the man in the picture gouging some poor bishop's eyes out. He was certain the bishop must have deserved it, but he felt a thrill of fear run up his back. "Why?"

"The reason doesn't matter," said the duchesse. "And, in any event, it is long forgotten. Only the brutal deed itself remains in memory."

Maurice stopped eating while she explained.

"Even if we were not obliged by duty to our ancestors to keep it, we would display that portrait to remind us of Hélie and his viciousness. The painter, you see, painted those pikes behind the comte deliberately. He wanted Hélie to appear as Satan. Hélie never thought it was any-thing other than an ordinary portrait. He did not under-stand that he had been ridiculed by his own portrait painter.

"A great family would not ordinarily tolerate ridicule by its servants, and in any other noble house the painting would have been destroyed long ago. But we want to be reminded of our ancestor's crime, because it is our burden of conscience. It is not the only crime our family has committed, simply the most vicious. Hundreds of years ago, the Périgords used this country in the most abominable manner: burning houses, mutilating livestock, robbing families, killing people."

Maurice was no longer hungry and laid the apple piece back on the plate.

"I daresay Auguste's ancestors were among the people your ancestors used so despicably," said the duchesse.

Maurice felt the hot breath of shame against his neck, as if he had been the one to destroy villages and mutilate livestock.

"Our people have ridden the backs of Auguste's people for millennia," said the duchesse. "Auguste and his people have lived through more pain than you can readily imagine."

"I'm sorry." Maurice looked up at the duchesse.

Her face was calm and gentle, despite what she'd been saying. "I am sorry as well, Your Highness. We are responsible for the behavior of our ancestors."

"What must I do?"

"You must always remember that nobility is a debt you can never repay. You must respect the dignity of every human being, and that means treating them like people and not beasts of burden."

Maurice felt sorry for what he had done. "I shall apologize to Auguste for riding on his back."

"Heavens, no," said the duchesse. "That would be undignified for you and embarrassing for Auguste. Act as if it never happened."

"I will not do it again," he said.

"You see how difficult it is to keep one's character clean and presentable."

Maurice did indeed see.

The duchesse smiled. "These are the last of the apples we dried last autumn, but the strawberries will be ripening soon. Your Highness will enjoy those.

"In two days, your father comes for you."

The excitement of the next two days, until Maurice's father arrived, nearly overwhelmed the boy. All day he practiced walking with his crutch, and as soon as he finished asking the Lord to bless everyone and to bring Archambaud, he fell into bed exhausted. He did not sleep, for his head buzzed with questions of what this father would think of him and whether he would tell him what it was like at court and when he could see Archambaud.

On the appointed day, Maurice asked Auguste to help him brush his hair and don his very best clothes. He had to direct Auguste most minutely, for the servant had no sense of good appearance in a man, and several times Maurice feared he might lose patience with him. But he remembered the lessons of the duchesse and spoke to him always with courtesy and respect.

It seemed to take forever to dress, but then they finished and waited in Maurice's room for what seemed hours before a servant brought word that his father was in the drawing room. He asked Auguste to help him quickly put on his leg brace and then he grabbed his crutch. Auguste carried him, crutch and all, to the drawing room.

Auguste set Maurice on his feet, and Maurice arranged himself with his crutch. The crutch seemed to him as large as he was, and despite his practice with it he felt awkward. But he did not want to be carried into the presence of his father. The door servant pushed open the door, and Maurice walked through, painful step by painful step.

Inside the room he found the duchesse seated in her favorite reading chair, and his father, whom he recognized from one of the portraits in the great hall, standing beside her. There were other people in the room as well, but such was Maurice's excitement that he took no note of them and whether they were seated at the proper distances from his father and grandmother.

Maurice's father was dressed in knee pants and hose, and black shoes with silver buckles. He wore a coat that reached halfway down his leg, after nipping in at the waist and flaring over the hips. Lace spilled out the front of the coat and from its cuffs. His wig was thick and bright white, and there were no signs of powder on the shoulders of his coat.

"Charles-Maurice, my son," he said. He did not smile as many of the adults did when they addressed Maurice, but spoke to him as if to another man.

Maurice admired him immensely and thought he compared favorably to any of the château's visitors, especially the bailli de Périgord, who called on the duchesse (as did every person of consequence) from time to time.

Maurice took several dignified steps toward him, aided by his crutch. The man's expression was impassive, but his eyes flickered ever so slightly, and Maurice felt warm inside at this expression of his father's affection.

"Greetings, Father," he said. Then, adopting his duties as chamberlain, he said, "Welcome to Chalais."

The comte smiled. "He welcomes me to my own ancestral seat."

Maurice smiled, too, pleased to have impressed him.

"You look well," said the comte.

"Thank you, Father," said Maurice. "Have you news of my younger brother, Archambaud?"

His father looked surprised. "Indeed I do. Have you been told then?"

Maurice knew then that he was going to meet his younger brother, and he was filled with excitement. God had heard his prayers.

"I have received the blessing of the King," said his father, "in naming Archambaud as heir. He shall be trained for the command of a regiment."

Maurice was so happy that he would have shouted, had he not thought it would be unseemly. "I shall be pleased to share my room with my younger brother," he said.

For an instant the comte looked discomposed, but he recovered himself before Maurice could ask him what was wrong. "Charles-Maurice, my son," he said, "Archambaud will not share your room. He is to assume the position of heir."

Maurice found it difficult to understand what he was saying. "But I have the grandest room," he said. He turned to his grandmother. "What room will Archambaud take, Duchesse?"

His grandmother said nothing. But Maurice saw a tear forming at the corner of her eye. Fear gripped him then, although he could not have said what he was afraid of. He turned back to his father.

"I do not understand, Sir," he said.

"You are to be enrolled at the College d'Harcourt," said the comte.

Maurice remembered the dark little room and the pictures of the sad men. "The College d'Harcourt?"

"I am sure you want what is best for our line," said his father.

Maurice leaned hard against his crutch.

"The aristocracy is diluted with families who have no

more claim to nobility than ready cash. Noblesse de robe."
He spoke the last three words with contempt.

Maurice heard what his father was saying, but he
could not make sense of it. He only knew that he was
being sent away from Chalais. The third lion, cast to the
bottom of the shield.

"Not the Périgords," said the comte. "We purchased
our nobility with blood and steel. We are noblesse de
l'épée, and holding the title means mastery of the sword.
So Archambaud will be trained to swordsmanship, and he
will assume the responsibilities of heir. You, my son, will
become a priest."

Maurice did not know what it would feel like to be a
priest. He only knew what it meant to be a comte, which
was all he wanted to be. The backs of his eyes hurt, so he
did not speak, for he knew this was the sign that he
might cry. He thought about his prayers to God to bring
Archambaud to Chalais, and it occurred to him that his
prayers had been answered.

CHARLES-MAURICE

FIVE

I HAVE SPENT MY LIFE studying people's desires and finding ways of aligning them with my own. Why should the maneuverings around my deathbed be any different?

Pauline and her mother want me to die in a state of grace. The Pope wants me to say I was wrong and the Church was right. I want the dignity of being buried properly, among the Talleyrands and Périgords, where I belong.

We can all have what we want when I sign the recantation.

A week from now, the Pope will receive this insipid document. If I play the hand properly, he will learn that I am dead and can revise it no further. Perhaps it will make him angry to be tricked, but he will not require that I be dug up again. I have learned over the years that you can rely on what principled men consider seemly.

A soft snore issues from the direction of Pauline's confessor. I look up and see that Father Dupanloup's head is thrown back, and he is asleep in his chair. I have been musing, and I suppose that makes me tedious company. But then, this is the last day of my life. In a matter of hours, I will be no company at all.

I fear dying, but I cannot say I regret it. I have lived longer than I might have expected to. The people I have known who are now dead could populate a good-sized city. And what a dangerous city it would be, for I have outlived not only my friends but my enemies and the killers of my enemies.

It has pleased many people — most of whom I have survived — to believe that, as a young man, I sold my soul to Satan. I have never discouraged this belief, for I have often found it useful. But, in fact, I never had the opportunity to sell my soul to Satan. When I was a child, my parents sold it to God.

Pauline is on her knees by the bed, and her head is bowed against her clasped hands. She is perfectly still. I suspect she has fallen asleep while praying. It is so gloomy and close in here that I am surprised she and her confessor have stayed awake as long as they have.

The door begins to open, and it scrapes softly against the carpeting. Father Dupanloup does not stir, and neither does Pauline.

The door swings open, and there stands the duchesse de Dino — Dorothée, Pauline's mother. We recently celebrated her forty-fourth birthday, but to me she is still the violet-eyed fifteen-year-old who captured my heart when she first came with her mother to my house. I knew from the day she arrived that she was the last woman I would love.

My life has had an interesting symmetry. It was a duchesse who guided me into the world at Chalais. It is a duchesse who guides me out of it here.

I have often wished I could have married this duchesse.

We only wish for what we cannot have, however. If the object of our desires can be had, wanting it is no longer a wish. It is a plan.

But I could no more become Dorothée's husband than I could dance a waltz. I was already married to Catherine when I met her, and by the time Catherine freed me by dying, I was over eighty.

Dorothée's husband, my nephew Edmond, never deserved a woman as graceful and intelligent as Dorothée. He is a fine young man and, as the son of Archambaud, heir of the Périgords, an important one as well. But I fear he has nothing to commend him other than a title and accomplished swordsmanship.

A title is always useful, but there is precious little call for swordsmanship these days. A generation of France's finest swordsmen lost their heads in the Revolution and were little missed. Some, like Archambaud, only survived by waiting out the Revolution abroad.

Our late Emperor, who put great stock in tradition, encouraged young men to wear swords, but they did not use them very often. After all, the Emperor's own specialty was artillery, and nobody ever stopped grapeshot with a blade. It is unfortunate, but swordsmanship is an art that has outlived its usefulness. And since nobility owes its very existence to the sword, the disappearance of swordsmanship is more than the loss of a pastime.

Dorothée and Edmond, although they were an excellent match for their families, never had any attachment for each other. From the beginning Dorothée lived under my roof and Edmond returned to his barracks and bivouacs. Dorothée has managed my household and entertained my guests for twenty-nine years. When Pauline was born, I allowed Edmond to stand in the position of father at her baptism, and then I sent him away again.

Dorothée glides through the doorway and around Pauline. She seats herself in the chair by the bed without disturbing the sleepers. I am glad she has decided not to kneel and pray. I would rather she conversed with me than with God.

Dorothée's large eyes are liquid by candlelight. She does not speak. But then, what would she say?

"You have been an incomparable lover and companion,

Duchesse," I say. "I am sorry you have spent your most agreeable years on one as unworthy as I."

She takes my hand, leans forward, and kisses my cheek. "I would not have spent them otherwise."

I know what many people think of me. I know the word "disloyal" is used in conversations about me. It is said I betrayed the Church, I betrayed the Revolution, the Directoire, the Consulate, the Empire, the Restoration. But how can one betray an abstraction? I have been loyal where loyalty has meaning: I have been loyal to women. It is a mean-spirited man indeed who would love an abstraction when there are women in this world going unloved.

Dorothée's large eyes glisten in the candlelight. She reaches over and strokes my forehead again.

I have loved many women, but a man must love best the woman who sits by his deathbed and strokes his forehead.

Pauline looks up. Her lips are moving, and I see I was wrong. She has been awake and praying. I am amazed at how intently and how long she is capable of praying. God must surely grow tired of listening to her.

She reaches over and gently tugs Father Dupanloup's sleeve. He looks about him as if gathering his wits.

"Please let the prince rest now," says Dorothée.

"But Mama— "

Pauline rises from her knees in a rustle of silk.

Father Dupanloup rises as well. "He has yet to sign the recantation, Your Highness." He reaches over and takes the recantation, then extends it toward me. "Will you sign now, Your Highness, before it is too late?"

I cannot sign until it is certain to be the last thing I do.

Dorothée saves me from having to refuse.

"He will sign once he has rested."

Pauline turns her lower lip out ever so slightly, then nods. She looks at Father Dupanloup. "Father, would you consent to hear my confession?"

Father Dupanloup agrees, and the two depart. Pauline confessed only yesterday, and I fail to see how she might have done any appreciable sinning since then. It would surely be a more lively confession if she listened to Father Dupanloup rather than the other way around.

Six

CHARLES-MAURICE found that in the corridor of life, one door after another was closed in his face, so that he was driven inexorably toward the altar waiting at the end, as if there were some intelligence directing him to kneel before the Church and accept the yoke of lifelong servitude. He suspected his mother of being that intelligence. She may have sent him away the day she met him, but that did not stop her from trying to dictate the course of his life.

He learned that she was the one who had decided he should leave Chalais. It was she who had decided he should spend a decade at the College d'Harcourt studying the lives of bishops and saints.

It seemed to Charles-Maurice that whenever he met with unpleasantness, his mother was not far away. Whether in person or through his teachers at the College d'Harcourt, she chose his friendships and encouraged his switch-wielding teachers to discipline him. She never came to the College d'Harcourt, but she required him to meet

with her and his father at their Paris townhouse once a
month for dinner. During these dinners, he was forbidden
to speak and encouraged to be a good boy of whom the
family could be proud.

When he was finally ready to leave the College
d'Harcourt, his mother decided he should move another
few steps toward the altar and enrolled him in the seminary at Saint-Sulpice.

For a youth of eighteen, the seminary was frightfully
dull, but it had two qualities to recommend it. One was
that it gave him respite from his mother. The other was
its location in Paris.

Charles-Maurice had lived in Paris nearly all his life,
but only under the watchful eyes of his mother's minions.
By the time he got to Saint-Sulpice, however, the dauphin
had grown to manhood, and his parents had even less
time than they had in the past. They gave him over to
the guardianship of the bailli de Périgord, who quite
ignored him.

It was like being released from bondage. As long as he
studied enough to keep from drawing attention, he could
do whatever he liked. And what he liked was actresses.
He learned that for a handful of sous one could stand in
the back of a darkened theater and watch them in all
their beauty and grace. Charles-Maurice spent his days
distractedly reading Greek grammar and memorizing the
writings of St. Augustine, but he spent his nights in the
single-minded study of actresses.

This study was limited only by his finances, for his
allowance did not permit attending the theater as often as
he wanted. He borrowed from his friends to supplement
his allowance, but he ran out of friends before he had
sated his appetite for the theater.

To continue his studies he needed money, and there
was only one place to go for money: his uncle. Charles-

Maurice hated the bailli, a feeling he had never told to anyone, not even Auguste. But he needed money. So one Sunday after mass he called on the bailli and was received in his study.

When Charles-Maurice limped into the room, the bailli stood from behind an enormous desk and walked around it to greet him. The boy had been in the presence of the bailli perhaps a dozen times in the course of his life. Each time he saw him, the bailli became smaller. Charles-Maurice delighted in this phenomenon. When he was younger, he had had fantasies of the bailli shrinking to the size of a child. In these fantasies Charles-Maurice would take away the bailli's sword. Then he would take the little man over his good knee and strike his bottom with the flat of the sword until the bailli cried.

Charles-Maurice dismissed the memory of this fantasy and bent down to kiss cheeks with his uncle.

"Studying agrees with you, nephew." The bailli walked back around the desk and sat down behind it. "The cassock makes you look more prosperous than the day I fetched you from your wet nurse, eh?"

Every time Charles-Maurice met his uncle, the bailli mentioned retrieving him from his wet nurse.

"Thank you, uncle," said the boy. "You are very kind. I am grateful to have the opportunity to study at Saint-Sulpice."

"You'll be a cardinal one day, eh? Become a statesman and bring glory to the family name."

"God willing," said Charles-Maurice. He suspected God did not particularly care about the glory of the Périgords, but it was a phrase that people in his family seemed to like hearing.

"Your note said you needed to see me on a financial matter," said the bailli. "Need to buy a hymnal or something?"

"I wish it were that simple, uncle."

"A new cassock? The one you're wearing looks fine to me."

"No, uncle," said Charles-Maurice. "This is a much bigger matter than that. You may be aware that Monsieur Tailleur, the clothing merchant, has died. His family pew at Notre Dame de Décor Sacré is now available, and I wish to purchase it in the name of the Périgords."

There was no Monsieur Tailleur, of course. And "Notre Dame de Décor Sacré" was a most unlikely name. But the bailli paid no attention to the affairs of commoners, no matter how wealthy they were, and he knew nothing of churches, as he attended mass only as often as he had been told was necessary to avoid torment in the afterlife.

"What? There is a pew in the name of the Périgords at the cathedral? What need do we have for this pew?"

"We have no need of it, uncle," said Charles-Maurice. "I wish to buy it for poor Monsieur Tailleur's family, who have been left with very little and are likely to lose it."

"You wish to purchase a pew in the name of the Périgords to give to some family of commoners? Are you mad?"

"Perhaps so, uncle," said Charles-Maurice. "Perhaps I am mad with the love of our Lord, who says, 'Give to the poor, and thou shalt have treasure in heaven.'"

The bailli regarded him sternly, and Charles-Maurice wondered if he had overplayed his meager hand.

But the man shook his head and smiled indulgently. "I shall never understand you clerics."

Charles-Maurice realized then that his uncle considered him a priest. It was strange to be considered a priest by a member of his family. He did not feel like a priest.

"How much does it cost, then, to have this treasure in heaven?" said the bailli.

"Only four hundred livres, uncle, and if you grant it, the Tailleur family will pray for you every day."

"You are serious about this, aren't you?"

"Oh, indeed, uncle," said Charles-Maurice.

"Very well, then." The bailli reached for a pen. "I shall write a letter to my banker. What is the name of the rector in this parish?"

"Uncle," said Charles-Maurice, "would you be good enough to ask your banker to pay me directly? I know it is vain of me, but I wish to gather the Tailleur family at the church and make a small ceremony of the purchase."

"You're a good boy, Charles-Maurice." The bailli wrote several lines on a sheet of paper. "I have never given this much money to commoners in my life." He blotted and sanded the ink, and then looked up at the young man. "Perhaps I have not always been the most Christian of men."

"I will pray for you, uncle."

"I trust this gift will improve my standing in the eyes of God." The bailli folded the note, then began to melt some sealing wax on it. He held the folded and sealed note out to the young man, and his eyes bespoke his sincerity.

Charles-Maurice was touched by his uncle's desire to please God. As he took the note, it occurred to him that there could be some advantages to being a priest.

In the street before his uncle's house, Auguste helped him into the carriage. He relaxed into the seat and felt the surface of his coat over the pocket where he'd put the letter to the banker. He avoided smiling, because he did not want Auguste to see him doing so, but he felt warm and pleased. Now he had the wherewithal to go to the Théâtre de l'Odéon and complete the purchase of his box. He did not know which he enjoyed more — the anticipation of owning a box or the accomplishment of having fooled the bailli out of four hundred livres. Perhaps he should have asked for five hundred.

🦁   🦁   🦁

With his own box, Charles-Maurice was able to attend the theater every evening, and it was from this box that the young seminarian first saw Angelique. He had come to the theater without changing out of his cassock. The performance was a revival of Molière's *Tartuffe* by the Comédie Française. Angelique played the daughter, and Charles-Maurice had never before seen a woman who combined such innocence and beauty. She moved like a rivulet and spoke like the first birdsong of spring. And when she stood with her hands clasped in front of her, her gaze down and off to one side, he thought she must be the very embodiment of feminine innocence. The young man was so enchanted that he abandoned decorum and draped himself over the railing of his box, watching her every gesture, her every movement.

At the edge of his awareness, he supposed the other people in the audience had noticed the display he was making of himself. But he didn't care. By the third act, however, he could see that the actors had noticed him. The actor playing Tartuffe actually began addressing his lines to Charles-Maurice, and he thought he could discern a certain amusement among the members of the troupe as they incorporated him into their performance.

After the performance, as the lights came up, Charles-Maurice took a pencil and a sheet of paper from his book satchel and wrote a letter to the young actress who so infatuated him, barely aware of the theater emptying around him. He described to her the joy of seeing her from his box. He wrote that she moved like a rivulet and spoke like the first birdsong of spring.

He had no intent of sending the letter. He just knew he had to provide some release for the feeling she had called up in him.

He finally made his way to the street outside and climbed into the coach, where Auguste was waiting. He was still bursting with feelings for the actress, and on the sort of impulse that only the smitten can feel he sent Auguste backstage with the letter.

Charles-Maurice sat in the coach in front of the theater for nearly an hour waiting for his servant's return.

Finally, Auguste appeared at the door of the theater, and Charles-Maurice beckoned him into the coach.

"Why have you been so long, Auguste?"

"She asked me to wait while she wrote a reply." He handed his master a folded piece of paper.

Charles-Maurice nearly tore the paper in his haste to take it. Then he leaned from the window of the coach and waved to a torch bearer to come closer so he would have light to read it by. He could hardly hold the paper still for nervousness. It took him some moments of shaking and squinting to puzzle it out.

Her reply said that she had seen him in his box. She apparently had noticed his cassock, for she said she had never entertained a cleric before. She would be pleased, the note went on, if he cared to call on her at her rooms in the rue Férou in one hour and hear her confession.

It was clear to Charles-Maurice that she had misread his intentions, and it weighed heavily on his heart. Not only did he feel it would be wrong to take advantage of the misunderstanding, but it seemed to him a sign from God that as he was studying to be a priest, he should learn to behave like one. Was it safe to defy God?

Charles-Maurice manfully decided to apologize to the young woman for his intentions and to clear up any misunderstanding about his capability of hearing her confession, and then to be on his way, ready to live out the priestly life that had been decreed for him.

An hour later, in a state of sadness, prepared to give up romance before he even knew what it was like, he approached her lodgings in a low building as unprepossessing as any he had ever seen,.

He announced himself to the servant girl who answered the door. "I am here to see Angelique," he added.

"But I am she," she said.

Her voice seemed somewhat similar to that of the young woman on the stage, but she was very much plainer than the person with whom Charles-Maurice had fallen in love. What should have been flax-colored hair was brown, and her drab dress was no better than one might see on a laundress. The cheekbones were lower on the face than he remembered, and her nose was wider. He leaned against his crutch and tried to understand.

"It is the make-up," she said. She smiled and, with a look of slight concentration, she grasped her hands together in front of her while she simultaneously looked down and off to one side in the posture of the daughter in *Tartuffe*.

Charles-Maurice was astonished. To think that the illusion of the theater was so powerful it could convince him that a laundress was the very embodiment of innocent beauty!

"Forgive me, Mademoiselle. I expected you to appear different."

She looked down at his bad foot. "And I you."

He noticed then a sparkle in her eye that was very charming, although it did not alter the rest of her features in the slightest. She invited him to make himself comfortable in her sitting room.

"Have you no flowers?" She sat in a chair about a foot away from him. "They usually bring flowers."

Charles-Maurice was surprised by the audacious way she sat so close to him, and he was disarmed by the question. "But— "

She would not let him speak. "Have you come, then, to hear my confession, Father?"

Charles-Maurice could feel his face reddening. "You should not address me as Father. I am only a novitiate. I am not qualified to hear confessions."

"Perhaps you will be qualified to *give* one tomorrow. You are a handsome young man, Aumônier." She leaned toward him, put her hand on his good knee, and squeezed it.

He could not understand why she would address him so, but the power of speech seemed to depart him altogether, and he could feel his face reddening.

She laughed loudly.

It was at once the heartiest and most innocent laugh Charles-Maurice had ever heard from a woman. He suddenly understood that she had been joking. He had never before met a woman who made jokes.

The infatuation he had for the character in Molière's play evaporated, but that evening he fell in love with the laughing Angelique.

She did not hold it against him that he'd brought her no flowers, and once he relaxed he was able to match her jokes with his own. He joked as quickly and as often as he could, for he loved her laugh.

She was laughing when she took him to her bed, and the two of them laughed over the learning of the buttons and fasteners of each other's clothing. When she was naked, Charles-Maurice stroked and kissed her small, round breasts until the nipples stood up. She tilted her head toward him and put her tongue lightly in his ear. He gasped with the surprise and excitement of it. Then she rolled him on his back. She straddled him and laughed her hearty laugh when he came.

Afterward, they talked softly in the darkness.

"How did you become an actress?" said Charles-Maurice.

"My parents."

"Are they actors?"

"No," said Angelique. "My father was an army officer."

"Is he no longer alive? Was he killed in battle?"

"When the war ended in America," she said, "they retired him and sent him home. They always retire the officers of common birth first. He came back to Paris and
assumed responsibility for the task of drinking himself to
death. It took him two years, until I was thirteen. After
that, my mother took in laundry. Because I was not shy,
and I have a good voice, my mother thought I could succeed as an actress. She made me go on the stage to help
support the family."

"Do you send her money?" asked Charles-Maurice.

"No," she said. "I am poor, and she is dead."

"I'm sorry."

"For what? Her death or my poverty?"

"I am sorry your mother is dead," said Charles-
Maurice. He didn't think money was very important.

"Don't be, Aumônier," she said. "In my neighborhood,
people die very early. My mother lived longer than most."

"Will you leave the stage now that your mother is
dead?"

"How can I?" she said. "I know nothing else. In my
neighborhood we get but one chance to make our lives.
My mother took that chance on my behalf."

"The same is true in my neighborhood," said
Charles-Maurice. "And my parents took my chance for me
as well."

Angelique laughed heartily. "You make sport of me,
Aumônier."

Charles-Maurice decided he liked the way she called
him Aumônier — as if she were a soldier and he a chaplain. He supposed it was a term she had learned from her
father. It sounded affectionate and informal, and he had

not been addressed by a nickname since he was a little boy.

They talked until they fell asleep.

Charles-Maurice awoke later, and he could see her dark silhouette leaning over him. He reached up to touch her breast. She took his hand and guided it to the spot between her legs.

"Touch me here, Aumônier."

She was wet there, and when he stroked the dampness she sighed with pleasure. It was the most exciting thing he had ever done. She let him do it for several moments, then she lay down beside him and invited him on top of her. When he entered her and began his movements, her body began at once to shake uncontrollably and she called for God. Charles-Maurice felt he was in the presence of a miracle.

Afterward, they slept again.

When the sun finally came through the single, small window to color Angelique's bedroom copper, Charles-Maurice realized he was hungry.

"Shall we have something to eat?" he said.

"You're welcome to a bit of wallpaper," said Angelique. "Or we could sauté some of the stuffing from the big chair in the sitting room."

"Do you joke about everything?" said Charles-Maurice.

"Most things," said Angelique. "It takes my mind off my poverty. But if you want something to eat, you'll have to go buy it. There's nothing here. I eat once a day. I think it is a good way to live, and it's all I can afford."

Charles-Maurice was still a young man and not ready to live that way. He gave some coins to a child on the street and had him bring them some rolls from a nearby bakery. Angelique agreed to share one. The rolls were unexceptional, but in the presence of Angelique it was the best breakfast he'd eaten since Chalais.

He had to return to Saint-Sulpice for classes, but he

was back the next evening, and this time he brought flowers. Angelique loved the flowers, but the two of them wasted little time over them and went straight to bed.

Charles-Maurice reached between her legs, but she took his hand away.

"What's wrong?" he said.

"That is not what I want right now." She propped herself on an elbow and faced him.

Charles-Maurice was astonished. Last night, it was exactly what she wanted.

"We have all night, Aumônier," she said. "Listen to me, and I will explain something to you. This is the age of reason, and we know the secrets of the universe are revealed to the one who finds the proper formula. Well, there is a formula for pleasing a woman."

"What is the formula?" he said.

"That there is no formula," she said. "A woman is not a clockwork device for which one finds the appropriate settings to set in motion her cycle of desire, joy, and satisfaction. One can only please a woman by learning what it is that pleases her, and learning when it pleases her."

She smiled at him and lay back down on the bed.

He began to stroke her carefully and gently on the shoulder, watching for any sign of reaction. She sighed when his hand approached her neck, so he moved his efforts there, spreading the caress to the side of her face and then her hair. He continued that way for the better part of an hour, caressing and stroking her and moving always in the direction that caused her to sigh or murmur. He was an explorer, searching for the undiscovered route to Angelique's pleasure. As he followed the signs, the sighs grew deeper, the murmurs became louder, and eventually he had her body shaking uncontrollably as she called once more for God.

That night, the explorer claimed the territory of Angelique in the name of passion.

❧   ❧   ❧

Charles-Maurice's life at the seminary became particularly difficult for him. Church history, theology, Greek grammar — they were all nothing but obstacles that stood between him and Angelique. In his classes at Saint-Sulpice, he struggled through conjugations and arguments, often growing hard under his cassock as he thought of Angelique and imagined new ways of exploring her body.

When he could get away from the seminary, he went to her and they made love. Every night with her was like a sojourn in Heaven before sunrise returned him to Purgatory, harder to bear each time because he had new discoveries of her with which to torture himself.

Charles-Maurice did not have the money to move her to better rooms, or even to pay the rent on her shabby little apartment. But she eked out a living from the theater, and he gave her presents as often as he could. He grew to love her dreary little rooms and threadbare furniture, and came to think of them as home. In the evenings, if she was not in a performance, he would come to her after his classes. Sometimes she would smile and drag him inside to make love to him like a tigress. But more often, she had the weight of the world and the drudgery of the theater on her shoulders. He would comfort her and make love to her gently and try to take her mind away from her life for a moment. For he knew what it meant to be trapped.

He studied her responses to every touch and every remark, cataloging and organizing them the way he should have been doing with the fine points of theology. He became an adept in the mysteries of Angelique. Giving Angelique pleasure, he came to realize, had less to do

with a particular caress or position than it had to do with
the care and concern with which he attempted them.

And after making love, they talked. Charles-Maurice
told her everything about himself. He told her about
Chalais and how much he'd loved it there. He told her
about the duchesse and the short-footed lion. He told her
how bitterly he'd resented his condemnation to the priesthood, something he'd never told anyone before.

She was widely read, although not well educated. She
knew nothing of the classics or of theology, but had read
much of the corpus of French drama. Notwithstanding her
practice of attempting to summon God when Charles-
Maurice made love to her, she was not a religious person.
She was, in fact, the first person he had ever met who did
not believe in God, and she had no particular respect for
Charles-Maurice's occupation. Whenever the subject of the
Church came up in their conversation, which was seldom,
she quoted Voltaire: "Écrasez l'infâme." Crush the infamous
thing.

This sentiment frightened him at first, and he half
expected to see her punished in some manner for uttering
it. Far from declining, however, her health and charm
grew apace.

He would sometimes help her practice for new roles,
reading the parts opposite hers. He watched the way she
delivered her lines, the way she tested the effects of different tones and gestures. There was no subtlety to her
acting. How could there be, when she must convince
people all the way in the back row of the Théâtre de
l'Odéon? Nevertheless, he began to acquire some of her
techniques, which he toned down for his own use in face-
to-face performances, such as those he put on to persuade
his teachers he had completed his assignments and would
deliver them presently. In any event, he had been raised
as an aristocrat and was steeped in the virtues of dis-

simulation. From childhood, he had been taught that putting on a different persona for the benefit of others was not only useful but polite.

However, he never put on a persona with Angelique, and he came to understand that he was happy with her. He was, in fact, happier than he could possibly have been with the flaxen-haired, innocent beauty he saw on the stage. It was the first time, at least since the duchesse, that he knew another person without the benefit of personas. He learned that the woman inside can be more interesting than the costume and the paint on the outside. He loved her without reservation or restraint.

His studies suffered, of course, but he became skilled at walking the line between minimal effort and failure. His instructors threatened him constantly with expulsion and even damnation, but he always managed to do just well enough to be retained. The other students were glad to have him as an object lesson, for it saved them from such service. He did not mind it. His position at the seminary had nothing whatever to do with Angelique and was therefore irrelevant to the purpose of his life.

Even in his final year at the seminary, he gave no more thought to his future than he gave to the mystery of transubstantiation. He thought only of Angelique. He raced from Saint-Sulpice to her rooms on the rue Férou every day, even during examinations.

. Angelique was not working the night before his last examination, and he refused to forego a full evening with her just to study. When she answered her door, however, she looked serious. He tried to put his arms around her, but she danced nimbly back into the room.

"How good of you to come, Father."

Charles-Maurice went in after her, assuming she was making another of her jokes. He was startled to find a man in her sitting room. The man stood. He was at least twenty years older than Charles-Maurice. He had a rounded stomach and was dressed in a black coat and breeches, with white stockings on skinny legs. In his left hand, he held a large black hat with three corners. He obviously knew nothing about the wearing of powdered wigs; the shoulders of his jacket were white with excess powder.

"This is my confessor," Angelique said to the stranger, "Father Talleyrand-Périgord."

"How do you do, Father." The man extended his hand as if he were Charles-Maurice's equal.

Charles-Maurice was too stunned to explain he was only a novitiate. He took the man's hand.

"This is Monsieur Boucher, the baker," said Angelique.

The man shook Charles-Maurice's hand and grinned as if he'd told a great joke. "I am an anomaly, am I not? Monsieur Boucher, the baker." He laughed.

Charles-Maurice smiled.

"My father and his father were bakers," said the man, "But with the name Boucher, we must have a butcher back there somewhere who took up baking."

Charles-Maurice was quite stunned by the situation, but his skill at making conversation assumed control of him. "It is unusual for a man to change his profession," he said.

"That it is, that it is," said the man. "It's not an easy thing to do, but it can be done. It's not as if you're called to butchery, is it?" He laughed again.

"I suppose not." Charles-Maurice looked from the man's grinning face to Angelique.

She had been watching him, but she looked away from his gaze and fastened hers on Monsieur Boucher, the baker.

"Where's your parish, Father?" said Monsieur Boucher.

Charles-Maurice did not know what to say. He looked back at the man. "Saint-Sulpice."

"The seminary? Do you teach there?"

"Yes," said Charles-Maurice.

"Tell me, Father," said Monsieur Boucher. "Do you know who bakes the bread for the students and faculty?"

"No, I don't." Charles-Maurice looked at Angelique. He hoped she might rescue him from further conversation with this philistine, but she refused to look back at him.

"My bakery can provide large quantities of bread at a good price." said Monsieur Boucher. "Perhaps you could remember me to the principal there. I am not hard to remember. Monsieur Boucher, the baker." He laughed again. "I am, in fact, difficult to forget."

Charles-Maurice looked back at him. "Yes. You are unforgettable."

"Thank you," said Monsieur Boucher. He slapped his hat against his leg suddenly. "I must be off. I leave you to your confession, my dear."

"Thank you," said Angelique. "Tomorrow then?"

"Indeed." The man turned to Charles-Maurice. "Nice to meet you, Father."

"Bless you," said Charles-Maurice.

"Thank you." Monsieur Boucher let himself out, donning his hat as he walked through the doorway.

Angelique closed the door after him.

"Is Monsieur Boucher, the baker, a friend of your family?" said Charles-Maurice.

Angelique turned back from the closed door to face him. "We must stop seeing each other, Aumônier. I am going to marry him."

Her remark was like a blow to the stomach. Charles-Maurice tried to speak, but he could not. He heard a carriage rush by on the street below and the cries of children playing hide-and-seek. "When?" he said at last.

"It doesn't matter when," she said. "I have accepted this bargain. I must begin to live with it immediately. You and I cannot see each other again."

"But could we not see each other from time to time?"

"I am not a comtesse who marries a man and then goes to bed with whomever she pleases," she said. "Monsieur Boucher and I are both commoners. It is not an arranged marriage. He proposed it and I accepted it. This will be a new role for me, but it's not acting. I will be a faithful wife. I owe him that."

"But why?" said Charles-Maurice. "I want things to stay the way they are. I have never been so happy since I left Chalais."

"I have been happy too, Aumônier, but there is no future for us. Even if you had the money, you could never provide for me, owing to your profession."

Charles-Maurice was stung by the accusation. "It is not my fault if I am to be a priest. They have done this to me."

"I am not talking about fault, dearest one," she said. "It's not important who put you in the seminary. The fact remains that you are there."

Charles-Maurice tried to speak, but she held up her hand and silenced him. "I must do this. I must leave acting, even if it means living as a baker's wife." She laughed humorlessly. "Madame Boucher, the baker's wife."

He attempted to embrace her, but she sidestepped him and walked across the room. "We will start our separation now. I am determined to be honorable about this. It is part of the bargain."

"But— "

She held up her hand again. "I hope you will be happy, Aumônier. But if not happy, I hope you will be warm and well fed and live in a sturdy house, which is really the best we can wish for anyone."

Charles-Maurice loved her more than he had ever loved anything. He looked around the shabby rooms at the grimy woodwork and the peeling wallpaper, and he knew she was right. He could not provide for her, and Monsieur Boucher was her best chance to live comfortably.

He tried to catch her eye once more, but she would not look at him.

He turned and limped out the door, taking himself into the night. He wanted to find someone who would listen so he could explain how unfair life was and how cruel God had been to him. But he did not know who would listen, and even if he found someone, he knew the third lion had but one thing to say.

"I do not complain."

SEVEN

CHARLES-MAURICE went to his examination, but his mind was on his misfortune. He had lost his home, his birthright, his title, and now his first love. He found himself wishing he were dead, and he wondered what it would be like if the wish were to be granted. He slept little, and he ate almost nothing. If Auguste were not there to help him dress, he would have attended his examination in his undergarments.

He managed to pass the examination, somehow. The seminary planned a small ceremony for him and his classmates to recognize the completion of their studies. Charles-Maurice missed the ceremony. Instead, he went to the theater that night and returned to his rooms afterward to drink two bottles of champagne and then fall into a deep sleep. When he awoke the next morning, Auguste gave him a note addressed in a feminine hand and sealed with

the crest of the Périgords. It was from his mother. She
requested that he attend her at court.

Charles-Maurice was inclined to ignore the invitation
on the simple grounds that he disliked his mother, that
he felt uncomfortable around her, and that he hated the
hypocrisy of wearing the persona of the respectful son.
But his grandmother had taught him that manners are
more important than principles and that the people to
whom he should be most polite were those he most disliked.

As if fulfilling a promise to the duchesse, he asked
Auguste to get him a fresh cassock suitable for traveling
to Versailles.

🦁   🦁   🦁

Even in his sullenness, Charles-Maurice thought
Versailles beautiful. The gardens were manicured, the corridors were spotless. And it had about it the refined hush
of civilized activity that he associated with Chalais and
his late grandmother. Oh, how he missed her.

But Versailles was much larger, more sumptuous, and
more overflowing with artwork than Chalais. Paintings,
sculpture, and priceless tapestries were everywhere. And
although the artwork seemed to come from every corner of
France and appeared to comprehend every style known to
civilization, each piece was thoughtfully placed so that the
overall effect was one of harmony. Each item fit so perfectly in its setting one could almost believe that placing
it had been someone's life's work. That may well have
been the case. The king's bathrobe and his undershirt
each had their own aristocratic curators. It was very
likely that every single item of furniture and decoration in
the small city that was Versailles came under the charge
of some cultivated man or woman with a title.

Charles-Maurice was not, however, allowed to enjoy the place on his own for very long. A lady of some refinement, herself attended by two other ladies, took him straight to his mother. His mother received him in a beautifully appointed chamber, and it occurred to him, as he limped across the carpet toward the small velvet sofa on which she was seated, that it was the first time he had ever been alone with her.

"How are you, Mother?" he said, for the forms of civilization are important, even in unpleasant circumstances.

"I am well, thank you."

She gestured to a foot stool near the sofa, and Charles-Maurice struggled to lower himself gracefully down on it. He sat before her like a child, which was doubtless what she intended. She wasted no time on the small conversation he knew she would have made if anyone else had been there to see it.

"Your father wishes you to be present at the coronation of the King."

Charles-Maurice did not roll his eyes, like he would have as a child, but the thought of the coronation made him wish to. He knew it meant spending several months of his life on ceremonies, rehearsals, and disgusting religious celebrations in the company of his parents.

"I am very busy with my studies," he said.

His mother's face was impassive, but he thought he detected a flickering in her eyes. They sat in silence for a moment.

"Listen to me now." Her voice was low, perhaps even somewhat menacing. "The Talleyrands have taken part in every coronation since the time of Hugh Capet."

Charles-Maurice wondered if a disinherited Talleyrand was still a Talleyrand. He had never even lived in his parents' house, and he failed to see what several centuries of tradition had to do with him.

"The vicomte de La Rochefoucauld, the marquis de

Rochechouart, the comte de le Roche-Aymon, and your
father have been selected for the signal honor of bearing
the Sacred Ampulla."

Charles-Maurice could not resist an ironic observation.
"The Sacred Ampulla must be very heavy that it requires
four men."

He thought he detected the barest sigh of impatience
escaping from his mother's lips, but he could not be certain, for her mouth remained closed and her face looked
like that of one of the statues out in the hallway.

"Your uncle, as the coadjutor of Rheims, will crown
the King."

If the Sacred Ampulla had its bearers and the
coadjutor of Rheims was to hold the crown, it sounded to
Charles-Maurice as if all the important responsibilities of
the coronation ceremony were taken. "What am I to do?"

"You are to conduct yourself quietly and with regard
to the forms and protocols of civilized society." Her expression changed then and took on signs of life. "It is a dramatic event, but it is not the theater. You are not to bring
a woman."

Charles-Maurice realized that his mother knew of
Angelique and his box at the theater. Should he have expected otherwise? She had been at court for at least
twenty years. She may be one of the half dozen most
powerful women in Versailles. She probably had servants
— and spies — everywhere. For all he knew, she was
responsible for Angelique's marriage to Monsieur Boucher,
the baker.

"After the coronation," she said, "we shall arrange to
have you attached to your uncle's office, where you will be
in a position to attend the archbishop while you work
toward your final vows of ordination."

Charles-Maurice knew he had done nothing to earn
this elevation. He was the last in his class at Saint-

Sulpice. Now he was to be the most powerful of its recent graduates. He was struck with the injustice of it, not that harder working and better students were being denied the opportunity of advancement that was handed to him, but that he should be punished so — condemned to a life of ritual and hypocrisy for no more reason than a misshapen foot.

"Thank you," he said.

"The only thanks I desire," said his mother, "is that your behavior should reflect well on the name of Périgord."

Charles-Maurice found himself willy-nilly a participant in the coronation of Louis XVI. And it was as he had foreseen: endless ceremonies, events, processions, rehearsals, rituals, celebrations. It was tiresome. He often had to stand for long periods of time, which was uncomfortable, and he was rarely in any gatherings with people of his own age. He had nothing in common with anyone he met, and he spent most of his time standing alone, smoldering like an unattended brazier.

It was at a function called the Dauphin's Last Ball that he was most miserable. He did not dance, of course, so he stood near the wall and watched the dancers bow and step in time to the music. The men wore brightly colored jackets, knee breeches, and silk stockings. The women wore voluminous reinforced dresses that completely hid them below the waist, and they all moved so smoothly they gave the appearance of being on hidden wheels. Men and women alike wore white wigs, and everyone was encrusted with gems and pearls.

Charles-Maurice, as befitted his station, wore a black cassock. He did his best to stand in one place, so as not to reveal his limp.

Part way through the evening, he was approached by someone his own age — a young man wearing a brocaded coat and a beauty spot on his cheek.

The young man introduced himself as the vicomte de something, the last part of his name being drowned out by the violas playing the current minuet. Charles-Maurice thought it would be rude to ask him to repeat his name, so he smiled as if he recognized it.

"There is a lady here who requires the services of a priest," said the vicomte de something.

"I am not a priest," said Charles-Maurice, who wanted to be polite but felt no need to impress anyone he met in this place. "I am only a novitiate."

"Please do not tell her that," said the young man. "She needs a priest, and she asked for you. Come along." With that, he turned and walked away.

Charles-Maurice felt he had no choice but to limp after the young man. He considered himself impolitely used, but that was no excuse for repaying it in kind.

The vicomte de something stopped before a lady who was seated with four other ladies. She wore a dress of gold satin that seemed to spill white ruffles from its every seam. Her companions wore pale colors, as if calculated to enhance the deeper color of hers. Charles-Maurice judged she was about ten years older than he. She had a remarkable edifice of white curls piled on her head, and it dripped jewelry, but Charles-Maurice's attention was drawn first to her sultry eyes and then to her pale bosom.

"May I present the duchesse de Luynes," said the vicomte de something.

Charles-Maurice saw she had noticed him gazing at her décolletage.

"Duchesse," said the vicomte, "this is Father . . . What did you say your name was?"

"Charles-Maurice de Talleyrand-Périgord."

"Oh my, an aristocratic priest." The duchesse de Luynes extended her hand. "Are you related to the comte who is the bearer of the Sacred Ampulla?"

Charles-Maurice took her hand. "His son." He touched the back of her hand with his lips. Her hand was warm and soft, and he did not let go of it.

"He will be in illustrious company." She made no effort to withdraw her hand from his. "The vicomte de La Rochefoucauld, the marquis de Rochechouart, and the comte de le Roche-Aymon are among the most important noblemen in the kingdom."

"My father is quite strong." Charles-Maurice gently released her hand. "And I am certain that if the King would only give him the opportunity, he could bear the ampulla by himself."

"Oh my," said the duchesse, "an aristocratic priest with a sense of irony." She looked at the vicomte de something. "Thank you, Vicomte. I am certain the duc will be pleased."

"A pleasure, Duchesse." The vicomte bowed and then departed.

The duchesse watched him walk away. "The vicomte wishes to receive the favor of my husband, the duc de Luynes," she said. "He is a sweet boy. I hope he is successful."

Charles-Maurice decided he disliked the vicomte. But he found the duchesse charming, and his gaze strayed back to her décolletage.

As she spoke, she made a gesture with her hand near her chest, which seemed rather calculated to encourage Charles-Maurice's attraction to that region.

"I asked the vicomte to bring you to me," said the duchesse.

"I am pleased your need for a priest is not an emergency." Charles-Maurice looked over her companions. "Everyone here seems quite healthy."

"Oh my, yes," said the duchesse. "We are healthy ladies indeed." She laughed, and all her companions laughed, too.

Charles-Maurice could feel himself smiling. The duchesse and her companions had dampened his smolder, or fanned it into flame. He was not certain which.

"This must be an exciting occasion for a priest," said the duchesse.

"A priest ordinarily tries to avoid excitement, Duchesse."

The duchesse laughed, and Charles-Maurice was gratified that she appreciated his irony.

"We get enough of it in confession," he added.

The duchesse laughed again.

"Oh my," she said, "you are amusing, Father. God must enjoy your prayers."

"Were we to pray together," said Charles-Maurice, "I would be surprised if He paid any attention to me at all. Even God must be susceptible to charm such as yours."

"Would you like to pray together sometime, Father?" Her hand went to her bosom again, and she stared at him boldly.

"When?" he said.

🦁　　🦁　　🦁

The next day, in the duchesse's private apartment, it was apparent to Charles-Maurice that she did not actually intend for them to pray together. Receiving him in her boudoir, she dismissed the servants and invited him to sit on a sofa by the hearth. No longer dressed for a ball, she gave a different appearance than she had the day before. The pile of white curls was nowhere to be seen, and her own hair, a soft brown, swept around her face in a fetching manner. It seemed the evening before that she had made her body conform to the shape and complexities of the gold satin dress. But this day she wore a simple arrangement of linen that seemed to impose no requirements on her but itself conformed to her body, which was slender everywhere except where it was round, namely, her breasts and bottom.

Charles-Maurice realized that she was not as old as he had thought. In this more relaxed and informal manifestation, she appeared to be his own age. He doubted he would have recognized her if she had not had the same sultry eyes.

"There is about you a feeling of tragedy, Father," she said.

"You needn't call me Father," said Charles-Maurice. "I have not been ordained."

"But you wear a cassock," said the duchesse.

"Not by choice," said Charles-Maurice. "I have been sent to the seminary by my family, who are ashamed of me."

He could not discuss these matters without a certain amount of feeling, and perhaps he allowed some of his pain to creep into his voice, for the duchesse gazed at him compassionately, then leaned over and kissed him on the mouth.

Charles-Maurice felt desire as well as sympathy in her kiss, and he responded with his own desire. Within moments, they were caressing and undressing each other on her bed. Once Charles-Maurice had removed his leg brace, he began to apply to her body the formula he had learned from Angelique. A caress here, a touch there, follow the sighs and murmurs.

He used his hands and his mouth on every part of her body, from the soles of her feet to her earlobes. In time she seemed to melt into desire and give herself over to him, as he moved his kisses and caresses toward her abdomen and then between her legs. Eventually, she began to quake and weep in the most violent manner, calling loudly for God and proclaiming her imminent death.

When she stopped quaking, Charles-Maurice entered

her and she began to quake again. It was but a moment before his own passion exploded. He rolled from her body and fell asleep.

He awoke with the duchesse twirling a lock of his blond hair in her fingers.

"Do the other women know about you?" she said.

Her voice had the tone of one discussing the prospects of a race horse.

"Know about me?" he said.

"That you have such skill," she said. "I have never been attended with such concentration before."

There was no affection beyond mere friendliness in her voice and gestures, but she nevertheless seemed to him well worth the effort of concentration.

"Are you going to go through with it?"

"Through with what?" he said.

She leaned toward him and kissed him lightly on the forehead, as a fine lady might do to her dog. "Becoming a priest," she said.

"Madame," he said, "I lack the physique for either dancing or swordplay, which are the only pursuits of the aristocracy. That is why I was disinherited by my family. Without an inheritance, I have no income. Without an income, I have no choice." He would not ordinarily discuss his personal life so openly, but there is something about nakedness, sweat, and orgasm that encourages such openness.

"Nevertheless," she said, "it is a shame to see a specimen like you donning the cloth."

They made love several more times that afternoon without much talk. It occurred to Charles-Maurice, in fact, that "making love" was a misnomer for what they were doing, for he could discern no feeling in the duchesse de Luynes beyond that of enjoyment. She was neither impolite nor unfriendly, but she was not affectionate either.

Other than the slapping and grinding of their bodies together, it was more like an afternoon of stimulating conversation than one of passion. He sensed a core of coldness in her that would not allow itself to be touched by another human being, and he wondered if she had been exiled by her family, too.

When he finally took his leave from her and limped from her rooms that day, she was asleep naked in her bed. With her sultry eyes closed, she had an innocence about her, and Charles-Maurice realized she was just a young woman thrust into a world that was comfortable but hard. He wished there were something he could do to make her life easier, but he knew there was not.

As he continued the endless rounds of rehearsals and ceremonies for the coronation, he saw the duchesse de Luynes several times. Her attitude was always friendly and polite, but he felt that if he had not actually experienced it, he would never have been able to tell that he'd spent an afternoon having sex with her.

However, she did introduce him to some of her friends. The vicomtesse de Laval, the duchesse de Fitz-James, the comtesse de Flauhaut — they all professed delight in making his acquaintance, and each asked to meet him in private. In these private meetings, the lady might be frank or timid, bold or shy, but he never had any difficulty determining why she wanted to see him. She always wanted to know what it was the duchesse de Luynes had been talking about.

Going from one fine lady to the next, Charles-Maurice felt rather like a tradesman with recommendations and endorsements. But he always endeavored to give satisfaction, for he knew it was the best way to get a good introduction to the next one.

By the time of the coronation, Charles-Maurice had bedded a dozen of the most aristocratic ladies of France. None of them even pretended to love him, but they were all grateful for his attentions. Gratitude was quite enough for Charles-Maurice, and he certainly enjoyed the process by which he gained it, for he knew now that there were few things in life he loved more than women. He loved to be with them, to talk with them, to have sex with them. At first the women were only a diversion from his troubles, but pleasing them soon became an end in itself.

Charles-Maurice never pursued a woman. But he became adept at reading them, and when he read in a woman's countenance the slightest interest in passion, he cultivated it. He found that the formula he used for pleasing a woman in bed was just as useful in her drawing room. There are gestures as good as a touch and comments as good as a caress. The sighs and murmurs one follows, however, are largely the same.

Just as he never pursued a woman, he never regarded the bedding of one a conquest. If he sensed a woman might be in the least diminished by sleeping with him, he simply did not do it. It was his rule that, regardless of custom, they should approach the transaction as equals and profit equally by it.

In the aristocratic society that descended on Rheims to prepare for the coronation, he found a substantial population of women who seemed to appreciate his rule in this matter. Many of them, in fact, remarked to him how refreshing it was to enjoy themselves with a man of his sensibilities. Thus did he pass the otherwise tedious time until the coronation ceremony.

🦁   🦁   🦁

Carpenters and decorators had been brought from Paris to Rheims for the coronation, where they built triumphal arches in the street and erected a long arcaded gallery leading up to the cathedral. The whole of the sleepy little town was cleaned, rebuilt, and decorated to the most exacting standards. It was June, and Charles-Maurice wondered how the local people, who were conscripted for the manual labor, managed to tend their fields.

His father seemed to be everywhere. He wore a great hat with tall black feathers, and he cut a figure nearly as impressive as he clearly imagined himself to be. His three fellow ampulla-bearers wore identical hats, and together the four of them gave the appearance of a small forest of black feathers.

Charles-Maurice was allowed to wait inside the cathedral with about a thousand other aristocrats while the coronation procession approached. He looked around at the elegant people, packed as closely into the cathedral as the books in the library at Saint-Sulpice. He saw a half dozen women he had recently had sex with, and he was pleased to note there seemed to be hundreds more he had not yet serviced. He caught the eye of the duchesse de Luynes, who was standing next to her husband, a tall man with broad shoulders and an impressive wig. She smiled a greeting such as one might for any acquaintance, then looked away.

The choir sang a mournfully sweet hymn, and the sound echoed under the great vaulted ceiling of the church. It was altogether impressive, and Charles-Maurice realized that to some people that ceiling must appear to be part of Heaven itself.

Then he could hear a fanfare coming from outside and the voices of the choir rose to a chorus. He saw a clump of black feathers enter the church, and he knew the Sacred Ampulla was wending its way toward the altar. As the procession neared, however, he saw that his father and his three companions marched with their hands on the hilts of their swords and carried nothing. They walked in front of a group of four other men, unarmed and obviously much less exalted, who shouldered the shafts of a litter bearing the Sacred Ampulla.

The bearers brought the litter to the altar and, the air filled with song, set it on the floor. His father then stepped forward and picked up the ampulla from the center of the litter and carried it to the coadjutor, Charles-Maurice's uncle, who stood at the altar.

Then the hymn swelled to a Te Deum, and Charles-Maurice knew the King was entering. First came the important people: the nobles who were closest to the King. Charles-Maurice did not know very much about the royal household, but he believed it was filled with aristocrats who bore titles like Master of the Bedchamber and Bearer of the Nightshirt. His mother was among these. She had attended the dauphin all her life and was obviously important to him, for she was in the third rank of the procession ahead of him.

After this parade of important people came the King himself, a man the same age as Charles-Maurice, although better fed. It was a warm day, but he was cloaked in white ermine. He walked behind his nobles with gravity, clearly aware that he was the embodiment of the French state. Hearing the music and seeing this serious young man, Charles-Maurice felt a swelling in his chest and a lump in his throat, and he was surprised that the spectacle could move him to this physical reaction. But he looked up toward the ceiling and listened to the heavenly choir and realized that this is what the spectacle was intended to do. He looked over at the duchesse de Luynes again, and he could clearly see tears sparkling at the corners of her eyes. He would not have been more surprised if he had seen the same tears on the statue of the Virgin behind the altar.

🦁   🦁   🦁

After the coronation, he went back to Paris to pack his things in preparation for moving to Rheims to serve his uncle. On his third day back, two messages arrived. The first was a sweet farewell from the duchesse de Luynes. Charles-Maurice was touched, the more so since sending the note was not without risk for her. She mentioned also that she understood how difficult it was to live without money, and she had taken steps that she hoped would ameliorate his condition.

He puzzled over that while he opened the second message, which bore the seal of the monarch, the newly crowned Louis XVI. This message said that on the recommendation of the duc de Luynes, the King granted him the abbey of Saint-Rémy in Rheims.

Charles-Maurice barely checked himself from shouting with delight. Apparently, his desire to make the duchesse's life easier was reciprocated. He felt a kinship to the cold-hearted duchesse that was closer than any family attachment.

He was invited, the note went on, to present this message to the bailli at Saint-Rémy to make arrangements for receiving the abbey's income of 18,000 livres per annum. Charles-Maurice's heart jumped. An income of 18,000 livres! It gave him what he most wanted: independence. He was so excited that he almost forgot to finish reading the message.

He did go back to it, however, and read the final lines.

> On the advice of your mother, whom we regard as a friend and the most gracious lady in our court, we make this benefice contingent on your ordination as a priest in the Roman Catholic Church.

The fine hand of his mother again. He may be independent, but no matter what his accomplishments, he would follow her design for his life.

Eight

In PLEASING A WOMAN, Charles-Maurice never asked for more than the enjoyment of doing so. Nevertheless, the women he pleased were as generous as they were able to be. And those with well-connected husbands, brothers, or fathers could be very generous indeed. The benefice of Saint-Rémy turned out to be the first of many. Charles-Maurice had still not been ordained before he had acquired at least half a dozen livings. He began to understand what a generous institution the Church could be. Priests may work like draft animals for pay that amounted to slavery. But when named to the benefice of an abbey, all one needed to do was collect the income from it. There were no responsibilities.

That is not to say that Charles-Maurice lived a life entirely without effort. He threw himself enthusiastically into the pursuit of more benefices, pleasing as many aristocratic women as he could contrive to encounter. But none of his livings required anything more of him than to be polite to the woman who was responsible for it. This posed no problem for him whatever, as he was a naturally kind person and anxious to put those around him at ease, the way his grandmother had taught him. Over the next few years, he moved gradually from a condition of simple independence to one that might be characterized as affluence.

He learned a great deal about Church finances in his

uncle's office at Rheims, but when he had enough money to live in style in Paris, he took his leave and moved back to the city. There, he had no more responsibilities than any of the young aristocratic wastrels who were so plentiful in the city. He became friends with many of them and came to be known in the city as the abbé de Périgord.

As he came to know more women, he could see that his reputation was beginning to change from that of a stricken young man — driven to the priesthood by circumstances — to that of a depraved hypocrite who used his position with the Church most abominably. The change in his reputation seemed to bring more women.

Among these was the comtesse de Brionne, who was the daughter of a prince of Rohan and the wife of the King's Master of Horse. In her boudoir, Charles-Maurice showed the comtesse that her passion ran to greater depths than she had imagined. He had never before encountered a woman capable of an explosion quite like that of the comtesse de Brionne — it went on and on for what seemed to be most of the night.

She was so exhausted by the experience she fainted dead away, and Charles-Maurice was concerned that she had died. But he studied her closely and saw a faint breathing was moving her exquisite breasts in a slow but discernible rhythm, so he lay down beside her and napped. It was nearly dawn when he awoke and saw her sitting up on the bed beside him. She leaned over and kissed him.

"This was an experience unlike any other," she said. "You are the most amazing man I have ever met."

"I am but a simple priest," said Charles-Maurice, although he had yet to be ordained.

"You should not be a priest," she said.

Charles-Maurice was afraid she was going to deliver a sermon about the priesthood and celibacy, but she surprised him.

"You should be a cardinal."

Charles-Maurice laughed. "I am delighted to have pleased you."

"You deserve a position commensurate with your abilities," she said. "I will make it so."

Charles-Maurice laughed again.

The comtesse de Brionne, however, happened to be a good friend of the King of Sweden, who was a good friend of the Pope. Charles-Maurice later learned that she wrote a letter to the King requesting that he recommend him to the Pope to be a cardinal.

He was astonished and gratified. Did he really have a chance of becoming a cardinal? It was a strange possibility to think about. He decided that his cardinalate would be different. He would not wear the scarlet robes, for one thing.

He did not get very far in planning his cardinalate, however, before word came that the Vatican turned down the King of Sweden's recommendation. Charles-Maurice was actually somewhat relieved. And he found it perfectly understandable that the Pope would not want to appoint a cardinal on the recommendation of a Protestant monarch.

Nevertheless, he had been very close to gaining a position higher than he had ever thought possible, all for unlocking a woman's passion. He began to feel that in pleasing women he had found the calling that had eluded him in his theology studies.

🦁　　🦁　　🦁

There was, however, one woman he was never able to please in any way, and that was his mother. She summoned him one afternoon shortly after he learned he was not to be a cardinal.

Charles-Maurice took a coach to his parents' house,

the same grand structure in which he had first met his mother when he was four. Limping after the servant, he looked around the corridor at the paintings and the furniture. His parents had made no changes here since they left Versailles to finish out their days at home. The dauphin was now king, and their presence at court was no longer necessary. His mother was nearing fifty — not ancient, perhaps, but too old to be ornamental. He thought about the unpleasant memories this place had for him.

He had never lived here, but he'd dined here with his parents once in every month for a decade while he was enrolled at the College d'Harcourt. His parents seemed to believe it was a treat for him. They always made it an occasion that centered on him alone, as if the presence of his brother Archambaud would detract from his enjoyment rather than provide him with some diversion from their tedious interest. So he sat at a table with his mother and father, and there was no one else there besides servants.

His parents did not talk with each other during these dinners, but they took turns asking him questions. Neither of them ever said anything about life at court or family affairs. They asked him about his studies and his interests and the events in his life. Every answer he gave was followed by another question. They were both consummate conversationalists, capable of feigning sincere interest even in the life of a child.

He found these dinners a torment. Even as he ate truffles or the most exquisite blanquette de veau, his mind dwelled on the fact of his exile from the family. And the way he was brought to them once a month, like a beggar brought to the house for a Christmas dinner, simply reminded him of how alone he was in the world.

Dinner always ended with the same admonition from his mother: "Be a good boy and do as the priests tell you to do."

He had not heard it in seven or eight years, but the memory of it was enough to fill Charles-Maurice with revulsion. He was not feeling kindly toward his mother by the time he reached the door of the drawing room, which the servant opened for him.

His mother was seated on a divan. She was alone — well dressed as ever, but the powder and rouge on her face did nothing to hide her age. It merely accentuated the fine creases that had begun to appear. Small, delicate folds now hung under her chin. It must be difficult for a woman like his mother to age.

"How are you, Mother?" he said solicitously. "How is my father?"

"Your behavior is a scandal," she said.

The accusation stung him like a carriage whip, not because he cared what people thought of his behavior, but because of the way his mother turned aside his greeting. His resentment flooded back, and he was unable to stop himself from answering with the most hurtful question he had.

"How is life at court, Mother?"

She looked like a woman who'd been struck. "Are you as cruel as you are iniquitous?"

He realized he had been cruel, and he regretted it. By long practice he allowed nothing to show on his face, but he was sorry.

She collected herself for a moment, then resumed her inquisition.

"In all your years of education, have you never encountered the idea of chastity? I could search the city of Paris for days without finding a woman you have not taken to bed. Have you no respect for your profession?"

Charles-Maurice prided himself on his conversation and wit, but his abilities deserted him. He could think of nothing to say.

"Well?" she said.

"What are you talking about, Mother?"

"Have I given birth to a liar as well as a libertine?" she said.

He realized he was going to have to participate in the conversation. "The weather is very fine for early spring," he said.

"Did you really think you deserved to be a cardinal?"

"It is a good year for planting."

"You are a disgrace to your family," she said. "You must change your ways, or we will all suffer damnation."

"The strawberries should be ripening soon."

"What have you to say for yourself?" she demanded.

"I am very fond of strawberries."

"Have you no shame?"

"I have always liked them," said Charles-Maurice.

By the time Charles-Maurice could gracefully take his leave of her, he felt a strange serenity. It must have been visible in his face, for she seemed more angry with him at the end of the meeting than at the beginning.

He was pleased to realize that he did not mind.

🦁   🦁   🦁

There were great things afoot among his friends. This group of aristocrats who fancied themselves intellectuals had conceived the idea of bringing Voltaire to Paris. The old man had spent the past twenty years at Ferney, just beyond the French-Swiss border. He'd been to the Bastille enough times that he preferred to pontificate beyond the reach of the government. But he was eighty-four years old, and the city seemed anxious to make its peace with him while there was still a chance.

The young, liberal-minded Louis XVI agreed to provide an assurance of safe conduct, and the old man was invited to Paris.

The city went into a veritable orgy of celebrations and ceremonies. Voltaire's poems, histories, and philosophical works were republished in new editions. The Comédie-Française began rehearsals of his tragedy *Irène*. On the day of his arrival, there was a parade in his honor.

The sage was installed at the townhouse of the marquis de Villette, and a committee of young men drew up a schedule that allowed him to greet up to a dozen people at a sitting, after which he retired to the bedroom in the company of his doctor to endure a coughing fit of sputum and blood.

It was Angelique who introduced Charles-Maurice to the works of Voltaire. As oppressive a place as Saint-Sulpice was, it had a wonderful library, and the young theology student had managed to read a great deal of the man's work. Voltaire was known generally throughout the city as the pope of impiety, but Charles-Maurice did not put a great deal of stock in piety, so he was not put off by the man's reputation. Indeed, he placed a great value on one of the patriarch's more famous sayings: "Worship God, serve the King, love mankind."

So of course he sought a place on the old man's schedule.

His efforts were rewarded in the spring, and he went to the Hôtel de la Villette with a rapidly beating heart. The great man's keepers had the situation well organized, and Charles-Maurice waited in a library while the members of the audience collected in order to be presented together. He was surprised that the rest of the group, who were all about his age, took the event so seriously. Everyone arrived near the appointed time, and no one made any attempt to cause other people to wait.

When they were all assembled, a servant opened a set of double doors into the drawing room, and the people in Charles-Maurice's group filed in by twos, arranging themselves in a half circle across the room from a seated man, who was easily the oldest person Charles-Maurice had ever seen in his life. He sat in a well-stuffed chair. He wore a dressing gown and had a blanket over his lap.

When they were all in the room and the doors closed behind them, Voltaire spoke in a thin but steady voice.

"If I appear to be uncomfortable, it is because I am," he said. "I am very old, you see. I should have been dead by now, but I stay alive in order to enrage those who pay my annuities."

The room erupted into gales of laughter.

Voltaire did not even smile. "I advise all of you to keep your health so that you might do the same. It is not like love, but it is a sweet pleasure none the less."

Everyone laughed again.

"And it never results in unwanted children," said Voltaire.

The laughter was even louder for this remark, and Charles-Maurice could feel admiration for this man welling up inside him. He may look decrepit, but he was a towering mind, and he radiated a spirit of generosity.

"I see there is a priest among you," said the old man.

Charles-Maurice endeavored to stay calm. "Still a novitiate, Monsieur."

"Come here," said Voltaire.

Charles-Maurice limped forward. He was used to looks of sympathy or curiosity when people saw him limp for the first time, but Voltaire betrayed neither.

"I was educated by Jesuits," said Voltaire.

Charles-Maurice could not resist an ironic comment. "How unfortunate."

He heard titters from the people behind him.

"Indeed," said Voltaire. "I have been trying to rid myself of priests my entire life. It is like trying to rid oneself of a birthmark."

The audience laughed again, Charles-Maurice among them.

"But now," said Voltaire, "I find myself in need of guidance from a man of faith."

"How could I presume to advise the greatest philosopher of the age?" said Charles-Maurice.

"You are a polite young man," said Voltaire. "My compliments to your parents."

Charles-Maurice answered without a thought. "My parents are dead, Monsieur."

Voltaire said something sounding sympathetic, but Charles-Maurice did not hear it. He was contemplating the possibilities in what he had said. Could he escape the control of his parents by simply acting as if they were dead?

He realized Voltaire was still talking to him.

"I will be joining them soon," said Voltaire. "Have you any advice for me?"

"Having never been dead," said Charles-Maurice, "I am in no position to offer guidance to anyone about it."

Voltaire's face looked at once surprised and delighted. "Then I have some advice for you."

Charles-Maurice felt warm inside for having excited the old man's admiration.

Voltaire smiled again, and Charles-Maurice was struck by how much beauty there was in that ancient, craggy face with its coarse features and deep creases.

The philosopher made a beckoning gesture.

Charles-Maurice stepped closer, then with only the slightest difficulty knelt at the old man's feet and bowed his head. He felt bony fingers on the back of his neck, and the room erupted in applause as the priest was blessed by the philosopher. Charles-Maurice kept his head bowed, enjoying the attention. He heard a rustling sound, and he realized Voltaire was whispering to him.

He strained to hear the old man, for Voltaire was the greatest thinker of the century and as he felt himself nearing his death, his words must be very precious indeed.

"It is important to be polite," whispered Voltaire.

Charles-Maurice searched the remark for some meaning, but he could find nothing other than what was there — that it was important to be polite. He had no doubt of the truth of it, but it sounded so feeble for a philosopher. He looked up and searched the face of the philosopher for the meaning of it.

Voltaire simply smiled.

"What do you mean, Monsieur?" whispered Charles-Maurice.

"I mean that it is important to be polite," said Voltaire. "I know it may sound banal, but the approach of a man's death doesn't make him any wiser. It just makes him scared."

TALLEYRAND

NINE

MY YOUTH TAUGHT ME to live on the surface of life. Pain lurks in the depths, down where the currents are cold and monstrous creatures wait. So I have swum and floated nearer the sunshine, and there I have met many others — swimmers who have been willing to play and splash with me for a time, but never to clutch too tightly to me, for that is the surest way to sink.

Catherine.

She had hair the color of spun honey, skin pale as moonlight, and eyes delicate and blue as delft china. She was raised in a French colony in India and spoke French with a charming creole accent.

She was not a woman of great intellect, and friends have asked me from time to time why I ever married her. But no one who had ever been to bed with her would have asked. I married her because I knew that if I married anyone else I would lose her — and the passion she brought to my bed.

And I loved listening to her speak.

But I must say the French language had played a cruel trick on her. When she explained to anyone where she was born, she said, "Je suis d'Inde." I am from India.

This statement always produced gales of laughter. Catherine was so sweet she would laugh along with everyone else. I suppose she never realized the remark sounded like *Je suis dinde*. I am a foolish woman.

I was required to marry, by the Emperor's command, so I married Catherine. The Emperor thought himself well within his prerogatives in requiring that the officers of his government marry. He considered himself a social and cultural hero as well as a political and military one. And he had definite ideas about French society and culture.

Napoleon may have forgiven the Revolution its executions and its massacres, but he could not forgive it the political influence of women. He was never well used by the other sex. He despised Germaine de Staël, whose intellect made him feel incapable of intelligent conversation. And as much as he apparently loved Rose de Beauharnais (Josephine, he called her), he was embittered by his discovery after marrying her that — contrary to appearances — she was both penniless and of undistinguished ancestry.

Ultimately, he avenged himself on the female sex altogether. The Code Napoléon gives a husband the same authority over his wife that he has over his children, which is to say, they are his property.

And the Emperor believed every man should own some female property. He was a great believer in the virtues of family life. Families produce children. Children become soldiers. And soldiers were the currency he spent on the battlefield in pursuit of his destiny.

Catherine and I were not inclined to augment the Grand Army with our issue. Perhaps if we'd had children, our marriage would have outlasted our passion. We did not, and it did not. But we were neither of us dissatisfied with the way it came out. Long after she ceased to be interested in me as a lover, Catherine took great pleasure in the life I provided her, especially in the ability to make people address her as "Highness."

"Catherine," I hear someone say. It is a moment before I realize it was I who spoke.

I feel a hand on my face again. I look and see it is my duchesse, Dorothée.

"She's gone now," she says.

"Who is gone?"

"Catherine," she says. "You called her name."

"I was musing."

"Do you miss her?"

"No."

"Was she not the great love of your life?"

There has been no great love of my life. I cannot even understand the idea, and I suspect it is some modern invention manufactured by those who are dissatisfied with reality.

I look about me. We are alone.

"*You* are the great love of my life."

Dorothée smiles, and I can see in her eyes that she knows me too well and does not believe me.

"Will you ask them to return?" I say.

"Of course."

Dorothée's voice is soft, but I can hear it clearly. I believe this may be one of the few benefits of dying — acute hearing.

She leaves.

Voltaire was right. Dying does not make you wiser, only more afraid. I want to sign the recantation now. I want to do anything that might make this easier, that will assuage the fear. I want to cry out my fear and ask for comfort from the living. But what can the living do for the dying?

Father Dupanloup can say some Latin phrases over me and anoint me. Will that light a candle in the inky blackness that waits for me? Or will it just make me feel fretful and a little wet?

Dorothée returns with Pauline and Father Dupanloup. They do not look happy, but they look so very alive. It is as if the three of them have come to the port to see me off. Will they stand on the shore and wave? And will they appear to me like diminishing specks as I head toward the horizon, wishing they could be with me because I am afraid to be so alone?

The living are so certain that they know what waits for dying. They know that when I sign the recantation, angels will sing and God will open the gates of Heaven to admit me.

But I am closer to Heaven than they are, and I can glimpse it. Heaven is not a place of light and music and joy. It is an abyss of darkness and emptiness where documents, and prayers, and sins, and faith change nothing, mean nothing.

"Oh, Uncle." Pauline takes the document from the night table. "We are glad you called us back. We are glad you are ready to sign." She holds the document out to me.

Father Dupanloup lends his voice in support. "His Holiness will be pleased."

And I think of the Pope receiving the recantation and judging it insufficient.

"Be patient with me," I say. "I am not ready to sign yet."

For it is my final game, and I will not lose it.

TEN

IN FIVE YEARS OF TRAVELING the British Isles and the American continent, Talleyrand had seen some wretched places. But Paris in 1797 was the most wretched of all. Rivers of mud flowed through the city's main streets. Great houses stood in shambles, and monuments to monarchy were overturned, in pieces, or missing altogether. Food shortages, public executions, and mass imprisonments had collected in a pall that hung low over the city. People on the street looked lost.

The Republic of Virtue had ended when Citizen Robespierre went to the guillotine, and the city seemed to heave a sigh of relief. Women gratefully discarded the modesty forced on them by Jacobin purity and began to decorate themselves with feathers, bare their arms, and expose more of their bosoms. Transparent muslin was the most popular material for dresses, and a raised waist and a turban or headband guaranteed the wearer's loyalty to the ideals of the Revolution by recalling the costume of republican Athens and Rome.

There were few carriages in the city, and most citizens found they had to walk to the theater. The theaters, after the long hiatus of Virtue, were packed every night with undernourished audiences determined to enjoy the years of diversion they had been denied. Those who did not go to the theater went dancing, and many of the city's deserted churches were converted into dancing halls to sate the public's appetite for amusement. The people seemed to be trying to distract themselves from the war, for France had found herself the enemy of every European nation, with the possible exception of the Republic of Venice. Every day brought casualty reports from one of the many fronts where French soldiers fought to protect the right of their compatriots to dress in gauzy muslin.

Talleyrand had returned to France and been appointed Foreign Minister of the Directoire (which had supplanted the Committee of Public Safety as the executive government of France) by his patron, Citizen Director Barras. His days were filled with negotiations and planning, but he spent his evenings on cards. Talleyrand enjoyed whist a great deal, even the whist of republican Paris, which had its own peculiar discouragements. Playing cards were subject to the same shortages as everything else, and sometimes it was difficult to pretend not to notice when one's host produced a worn and greasy deck that should have been retired before the Declaration of the Rights of Man. People played these disagreeable cards in a state of distraction, with conversation devoted more to the price and availability of linen than to politics and society.

The evening Talleyrand found himself partnered with Montrond's wife was as tiresome as any he could remember. She was scatterbrained under the best of circumstances, but that night Madame de Montrond was preoccupied as well. The combination made for some frightful card playing.

Spades were trump, and Talleyrand was holding the ace. After a well-timed finesse, he knew Montrond was holding the king. He created a plan for getting Montrond's king on the table that would require at least three distinct plays, for he believed the most exciting trick in whist is not the one on the table, but the one that unfolds later, in accordance with your plan.

Talleyrand took the first trick and threw down his

card for the second. He thought his plan must be clear by then, and he expected Montrond to look alarmed. But he saw nothing on his friend's face but the look of a man sharing a joke with someone.

Germaine de Staël looked at Talleyrand, smiled knowingly, then threw her card.

"Our bishop has a plan," she said.

Talleyrand had not been a bishop since his excommunication, but Germaine thought it a great joke to address the Church's most notorious living enemy as "bishop."

Talleyrand laughed politely, but his mind was on the success of his plan. He loved to win at whist, and he could hardly keep his face from betraying his pleasure at the way the game was following his plan. Despite Montrond's amused expression, Talley rand was certain his friend would lose the king of trumps at the end of a succession of tricks that depleted his best cards.

But Talleyrand's partner, Madame de Montrond, ruined the strategy by throwing the queen of spades.

Talleyrand thought uncharitably of the thousands who had gone to the guillotine for conspiring to defeat the Revolution. In all that time, had no one proposed a law that would make incompetence at whist a capital offense?

Montrond laid down his king and smiled at his wife. "It's a pity to spend one's highest trump card, only to lose the trick."

His wife looked at him as if he had taken her patrimony rather than her high card. "Spending cards is perhaps preferable to spending one's fortune on a husband's debts," she said.

A silence rolled across the table like fog on a battlefield. One did not discuss domestic disputes over cards. Madame de Montrond could hardly have caused more consternation if she had opened a vein. But Montrond looked unperturbed, and Talleyrand wondered what secret must be sustaining his self-assurance.

After this incident, the evening went from bad to worse. More foolish plays from Madame de Montrond, more caustic remarks. And one of Germaine's guests, a gossipy woman at the next table whose name Talleyrand never caught, insisted on telling stories about the Terror, so that he caught bits and snatches of information that clutched at his mind like street offal might stick to one's shoe.

"He was denounced by another baker," she said. "And when they read his name out in court, everyone laughed so loudly that his testimony couldn't be heard, and when he went to the guillotine, and the bailiff read his name out, the crowd laughed so loudly no one could hear his last words. The poor man went to his death for nothing more than a funny name. Well, it wasn't a funny name, really. It was just funny for who he was. Can you imagine a baker named Boucher? It really is rather droll, isn't it? Although it's quite a tragedy that the poor man died for it."

Talleyrand noticed that Germaine was winking at him, which was their signal that she would like his help in clearing her salon. Talleyrand stood from the card table.

"I meet with the Directoire in the morning," he said. "I must go home and sleep. Thank you for a delightful evening, Madame." He smiled at Germaine.

Other guests began to stand at their tables as well, and the room filled with the sounds of people commencing the business of departure. Everyone looked tired, except Talleyrand's partner for the evening, Madame de Montrond, who looked . . . well, murderous. But Talleyrand was not thinking about poor Montrond. He was thinking about the gossipy woman and her story.

He approached her. "Excuse me, Madame."

She looked up at him. "Oh, Monsieur de Talleyrand. What can I do for you?"

"I could not help overhearing your story about Citizen Boucher, the baker," said Talleyrand. "Do you know what happened to the poor man's family by any chance?"

"Yes, indeed," she said. "The widow took her sons to America, and no one heard from her again."

"Thank you," said Talleyrand. "It is a shame the way great political movements break up families."

"Yes," she said, "isn't it."

He saw Montrond, who still had not risen from his chair. His friend was staring at him with a most mischievous look on his face. Talleyrand excused himself from the gossipy woman and walked around the corner of the table to Montrond, using the gliding step he had perfected to make his cane look more like decoration than support.

Montrond rose.

Talleyrand shook his friend's hand. "Good night. Please call on me whenever you feel the need."

The sympathy was apparently wasted, for Montrond still looked like the curator of a private joke. "I suspect you will be engaged," he said.

In the flurry of farewells and cloak donning, Talleyrand was not able to press further and find out what his friend might have meant by the remark.

Cryptic remarks annoyed him, especially after an evening of bad cards. All the way home he watched the dark, wet streets from the window of the lurching carriage the Directoire provided its foreign minister in deference to his bad foot.

Angelique was in America with her sons. He had not known that she had sons. It was a shame about Monsieur Boucher, the baker. Well, he was not the only innocent man to go to the gallows during the Terror. Who knows? He may not have been innocent at all.

Talleyrand had not thought about Angelique in decades. In the weeks and months after he had lost her, he would never have thought that possible. But when one

survives a wound, it heals. He no longer resented the
world for taking her away from him. He was, in fact,
thankful to have known her and to have received from
her that priceless gift: the formula for pleasing a woman.

The coach hit a loose cobble, and he was bounced from
his seat into the air. He reseated himself with difficulty.
He wondered how long it would be before Paris returned
to normal. When would he ride in a stylish carriage
again?

His annoyance mounted when his driver was unable
to take him directly to his front door. The porte cochère
was occupied by a heavily laden carriage, much grander
than his own. He worried that perhaps one of the Directors had come to see him. This was distressing. He was
tired, and he wanted to go to bed.

Auguste met him at the door and took his cloak.

"There is someone here to see you, sir."

"The owner of the equipage in front?"

"She says it is urgent." Auguste draped the cloak over
one arm. "She is in the library and has been here for
hours."

"She?" said Talleyrand. "A woman?"

"Yes," said Auguste. "I let her stay because she
brought an introduction from Monsieur de Montrond."

Talleyrand knew he must see the woman, at least as
a courtesy to poor Montrond. "Has she been fed anything?"

"Quite a bit, actually," said Auguste. "The lady has a
remarkable appetite."

"You may go to bed now, Auguste. I will see her and
take care of this myself. I will want a drink before retir-
ing. Is there any champagne in the library?"

Auguste nodded and went off with the cloak to
wherever it was he went with such things.

Talleyrand stepped quietly into the library. None of

the lamps were lit, and the only light came from the fire
in the hearth. In one of the large, comfortable chairs by
the fire there was a shape. But all he could make out was
a voluminous wrap and the top of a hood protruding
above the back of the chair. On the small table next to
the chair there was a tray with a plate and a wineglass
on it. The glass was empty. The plate had only crumbs.
He stepped closer and saw a glint from the vicinity of the
floor. It was her shoes, which barely peeked from beneath
her gown. The toes had gold tips. Above the shoes was a
gauzy hem, shot with gold thread that sparkled in the
light of the fire.

He stepped closer, and the form did not move.
Talleyrand realized she had fallen asleep by the fire.

He moved around to stand by the fire and look at her.
Her face was lost in the shadow of her hood, and the rest
of her was hidden by a satin cape. He cleared his throat,
but she did not move.

"Madame," he said.

It was as if he'd set off a small explosion. She popped
from the chair like a projectile. Her hood and cape cas-
caded into a pile on the chair behind her. Her eyes were
round and startled as a doe's. A mass of blond hair in
slight disarray bloomed around an exquisite face the color
of crème fraîche. Talleyrand judged her the most beautiful
woman in Paris; he was quite certain of it, for he had
made the acquaintance of an appreciable proportion of the
city's most beautiful women.

Full, red lips pursed, and her mouth loosed a single
sound.

"Oh."

Seeing her rise from the cascading cape before him,
Talleyrand felt as if he'd witnessed the blooming of a
flower.

They stood staring at each other for a moment, until
finally she spoke again.

"Please accept my apologies," she said. "The fire was so pleasant, and I have had such a long day. I fell asleep."

"There is no need to apologize," he said. "I have had a long day myself, and I understand."

"Monsieur de Talleyrand," she said, and her eyes widened with fear and helplessness. "I have come to ask a service of you. It is most urgent."

Talleyrand had to admit that her distress was appealing. He would have rendered any service of which he might conceivably be capable, but he thought it best not to make such an offer yet. He nodded for her to go on.

"I am Catherine-Noël Worlée Grand." She had an endearing and languid accent, which Talleyrand judged was creole. She pronounced the final name, however, with a hard ending that did not sound French.

"Grand?" Talleyrand tried to imitate the hard sound.

"My husband is English."

"Where is your husband, Madame Grand?"

"India, I suppose. I have not heard from him for years. Please, Monsieur, this is most urgent. Monsieur de Montrond said that you were the only man in France who could help me."

"Please," he said. "Go on."

"You find me, Monsieur, in the act of leaving Paris."

"Do you find it as dull as I do then?"

"Oh no," she said. "I am leaving because the police suspect me. Monsieur de Montrond was good enough to alert me that I am on a list of people to be arrested."

"You don't look like a criminal," said Talleyrand.

"It is all a misunderstanding, Monsieur. I have been corresponding with old friends who now live in England."

Talleyrand had such "old friends" himself — émigrés too tainted by, or attached to, the past glories of the Ancien Regime to attempt returning to France. The government was extremely suspicious of such people, but they had about as much chance of coming here to reverse the Revolution as Louis XVI had of retrieving his head. Talleyrand judged that the rest of her story might take some time.

"Please be seated again, Madame. With your permission, I will be as well." He sat in the chair opposite her.

"I have quit my Paris residence," she said. "I believe I must either go to England or to prison. I spent this afternoon with Monsieur de Montrond, who is an old friend. We had many things to discuss, and by the time we were ready to part, it was past closing time at my bank."

Talleyrand wondered why Montrond had never mentioned her before. But, more than that, he wondered how this young woman and Montrond had spent their afternoon. Knowing would doubtless shed some light on Montrond's peculiar attitude at Germaine's whist table this evening. He dismissed this thought as lacking in gallantry.

"Now I fear that I will lose everything," she said. "Monsieur de Montrond told me that General Bonaparte has assembled an army for the invasion of England and that tomorrow the banks would be looted. He told me there was only one chance for protecting my modest assets. He said I must seek you out and beg your help."

If General Bonaparte was planning an invasion of England, he had shared these plans with neither the Directoire nor its foreign minister. Talleyrand knew from experience that Montrond was quite a convincing liar. But why had he amused himself by using his gift to distress this young woman so?

"Can you help me?" She looked as if she thought him capable of protecting her.

It was gratifying.

And then he understood that Montrond, having finished with her, meant to send him this woman as a gift.

His first impulse was to ring for Auguste and dispatch him with a letter of gratitude to his old friend.

But he reconsidered when he saw that the fear in her eyes was genuine. It seemed to him insensitive to cause a human being such fear, and besides, Talleyrand was not certain he liked the idea of men giving women to other men as presents. It was hardly in keeping with the lofty ideals of the Revolution.

"I will help you in any way I can," he said.

The fear appeared to leave her completely. She relaxed, melting in the most fetching manner into the chair. "Oh thank you, Monsieur. Thank you." She smiled, and the smile brightened her face almost exactly as if the fire had flared.

Talleyrand could not help but feel gratified that his assurances were capable of banishing a woman's fear so thoroughly. "We will discuss your situation, and then tomorrow I will call on some people to get this straightened out."

"Thank you, Monsieur," she said. "It is more than I could have hoped for." But she made no move to leave the chair.

"Madame," he said, "have you a place to go tonight?"

"No, Monsieur. I have quit my residence."

"You are welcome to stay here," he said.

"Oh, may I?"

"I would never forgive myself," he said, "if I permitted you to travel the streets in the dead of night."

"I hope that I might find some small way to repay your kindness," she said.

"I am certain you will," said Talleyrand.

One must treat people in accordance with the ideals of the Revolution, but that did not mean living like a monk.

Talleyrand and his guest spent the night in her room. She suggested they not wake the servants, and knelt by the bed to help him remove his leg brace herself. By the time it was lying on the floor beside the bed, she was calling him, with a great deal of affection, "Shortfoot."

Surprisingly strong, she pushed him over on his back and began to explore him with her hands and mouth in just the way he had intended to do to her. But every time he attempted to take the initiative, she pushed him back down and continued with her caressing, stroking, kissing, sucking. Talleyrand wondered briefly where she had learned these techniques; surely not from her English husband. He grew almost painfully hard, in a way that had not happened to him for decades. When finally he was able to push her off and onto her back, he came almost as soon as he entered her.

He felt embarrassed for having come as quickly as a boy, but Catherine was neither disappointed nor unsurprised. She acted as if she expected a man to lose control and ejaculate within seconds of starting to make to love to her. Given her techniques for preparing him, perhaps that was generally the case.

Talleyrand recovered himself after a few moments and began to caress her with his hands. She seemed surprised, but at his insistence she accepted his attentions. He wondered if perhaps no man had ever attempted to give her pleasure. A touch here, a caress there, and follow the sighs and murmurs. She was not difficult to read. He applied his mouth to her most responsive places.

She tried to stop him several times, but he would not be deterred. He stroked and kissed and caressed and licked for what seemed hours, until she finally began to shake and cry and moan. And when the shaking slowed and finally stopped, and he gradually ceased his caresses, she began to cry.

"I love you," she said.

Talleyrand believed her, and at that moment he loved her as well. So he told her.

They made love again.

He finally had to drag the leg brace behind him while he limped back to his own bed shortly before dawn, just so he could get some sleep. He slept late the next day, and he could see bright sunlight peeking around the window curtains when he rang for his valet.

By the time he was out of bed and dressed, he knew the Paris banks had been open for some time. He sent Auguste out to the street for rumors and newspapers, then sent the upstairs maid to see if Catherine was awake and to ask her to meet him in the conservatory. The conservatory was one of the most pleasant rooms in his house, particularly when the autumn sun of early afternoon poured through its great windows.

On his way to the conservatory, he stopped at the kitchen and asked the cook to lay out something for his guest. The cook was unprepared for the request, since Talleyrand himself never took breakfast. It was the Foreign Minister's habit to eat but one meal a day, which was dinner. But Talleyrand knew his cook to be a resourceful young man, and proceeded to the conservatory without concern.

When Catherine arrived at the conservatory, she looked as beautiful in the sunlight as she had looked by firelight the night before.

Talleyrand greeted his guest and seated her before a plate of pastries and a dish of sliced apples and pears. She was exceedingly pleasant, although she did not speak very much before she had eaten every crumb of the food. Auguste's assessment of her appetite had been accurate.

"Have you plans for the future?" said Talleyrand when the plate was quite empty.

"I have not thought very much about it." With a napkin, she dabbed at the corner of her exquisite mouth. "Are there any more pastries?"

Auguste entered and wordlessly laid two newspapers on the table.

"Auguste," said Talleyrand, "what is the news of the Paris banks?"

"All are open and doing business as usual, Monsieur," said Auguste.

"Has there been no looting, then?" said Talleyrand.

"No." Auguste turned to leave, but Catherine stopped him.

"Are there any more pastries?"

"I will ask the cook, Madame." Auguste bowed out of the room.

The two of them chatted while they waited for Auguste to return, and Talleyrand suggested that Catherine leave her money in the bank where, he assured her, it would be safe, and to stay another day at his house. She agreed.

The foreign minister then excused himself, for the day was more than half gone, and he wanted to call on the Minister of Police.

He had papers to review during the carriage ride to the police ministry, but they lay unread on the seat beside him as the carriage rocked him into a reverie.

Some men plan their lives like a game of whist. But while Talleyrand loved devising strategies for card games, he had never planned his own life. For his personal affairs, he much preferred to allow events to unfold and then take advantage of whatever opportunities presented themselves. To the extent he planned his life at all, he planned merely to get himself into positions that would present opportunities. That was why he had taken on the Church's financial work when he was a bishop. It was why he had sought to become foreign minister to the Directoire, which was an office in constant contact with princes and heads of state. They were people with infinite resources at their disposal, who always seemed to want something from the Directoire. And the foreign minister was usually in a position to provide what they wanted, if he could be persuaded. It occurred to him that in the past few months he had become a reasonably rich man by allowing himself to be persuaded.

Talleyrand realized with a start that he had been thinking about himself. It was something he rarely took the time to do. What had come over him? He was forty-three years old, and the previous night in bed he had behaved like a man of twenty. Catherine was more than the most beautiful woman he had ever seen, she was an elixir.

The Minister of Police, whose kindly expression and manner belied his profession, seemed awed by the appearance of the famous Talleyrand at his offices.

He sent a clerk to get coffee and invited Talleyrand to sit down.

"How do you prefer your coffee, Citizen?" The Minister of Police used the Revolutionary form of address without irony, but then he seemed a man incapable of irony. He seated himself behind a desk as large as the ones used by the Directors.

"Black as the devil," said Talleyrand, "hot as hell, pure as an angel, sweet as love."

The Minister of Police allowed his mouth to gape for a moment before speaking. "How poetic," he said at last. He looked from Talleyrand to his clerk in the doorway. "You heard the Minister. Fetch it quickly."

The Minister of Police then took a sheet of paper and a pen. "A marvelous epigram, Citizen," he said. "I had heard stories of your legendary wit, but I must say it is delightful to experience it."

"It is delightful to be offered coffee." Talleyrand noticed the Minister of Police was writing something on the paper.

"How was that again? 'Sweet as. . . ' "

"Love," said Talleyrand. "Sweet as love."

"Ah, yes. Thank you." The Minister of Police finished writing, then set his paper aside and clasped his hands on the desk in front of him. "To what do I owe the honor of your presence, Citizen Minister?"

Talleyrand wondered what the man was going to do with his remark. Use it himself in conversation?

"I have come to begin a program of cooperation between the Foreign and Police Ministries," he said. "I thought that if we two worked more closely together, it might benefit us both."

"This is an excellent idea, Citizen Minister," said the Minister of Police. "I have longed for conversation about the affairs of my office with someone I might consider my equal."

Talleyrand hoped the man did not actually consider him an equal, but he felt prepared to treat him as one. This was, after all, Year Six of the Revolution.

The clerk brought the coffee and set out two cups for them, then poured it. The Minister of Police dismissed the clerk peremptorily. "It is so difficult to engage good help," he said as he began drinking greedily from his cup.

"Indeed, Citizen Minister." Talleyrand sipped the coffee. It was not pure as an angel. It was hardly pure as a brigand. "But this coffee is marvelous!"

The Minister of Police beamed as if Talleyrand had congratulated him on his police work. "We try to maintain the amenities, even in the face of shortages."

"You have succeeded brilliantly," said Talleyrand. A touch here, a caress there, and follow the sighs and murmurs.

"Thank you," said the Minister of Police.

They sat smiling and sipping coffee in silence for a moment.

"Have you, in your work," said Talleyrand, "encountered a woman from India?"

"Ah," said the Minister of Police, "you mean Citizeness Grand?"

"It would be easy to remember a woman coming from India, I am sure."

"Citizen Minister," said the Minister of Police, "what man could ever forget her?"

The Minister of Police told Talleyrand that Catherine was of English descent and that she had been corresponding with an émigré, a vicomte named Lambertye.

Catherine was French by birth, but Talleyrand did not correct the minister. He reflected that in corresponding with her vicomte, she was committing no greater crime than was daily committed by nearly every literate and well-connected person in France. It was impossible to imagine her in any kind of conspiracy. She might have the freshest skin and breath and the sweetest disposition of any woman he'd ever known, but she lacked the intelligence for conspiracy. She was innocent enough to write letters to anyone who showed her kindness. If she had moved in a different circle, she might be corresponding with the Tsar of Russia rather than some defunct vicomte.

Talleyrand could not finish the vile coffee, but he continued to raise the cup to his lips from time to time.

The Minister drained his cup completely. He prattled about the difficulty of subordinates who seemed to take the whole idea of *égalité* too literally. Then he began discussing spies, and it was he who brought up Madame Grand again.

"Is there a chance her correspondence with émigrés is simply an innocent exhange of letters?" said Talleyrand. "I suspect your ministry would be quite overworked if you had to investigate everyone in France who writes letters abroad."

"That is why I am asking the Directoire for more help." The minister's expression was without guile.

Talleyrand realized the man was a genuine child of the Revolution, doubtless elevated from a position of clerk or schoolteacher in the ancien régime. He probably did not know anyone outside France and therefore could not imagine writing letters to send abroad.

"Have you in the Foreign Ministry had difficulties engaging workers who understand they are indeed workers and not chevaliers?" said the minister.

Talleyrand continued to chat with him, but he came to understand the Minister of Police — notwithstanding his aspirations to social distinction — had gained his position through amiability rather than intelligence. It was difficult to persuade him of anything. Talleyrand decided to make use of the man's aspirations.

"May I speak to you in confidence?" he said.

The Minister of Police looked around the office. "Yes, of course, Citizen Minister."

"The Indian woman, Citizeness Grand." Talleyrand hesitated, giving the impression he was searching for the right words. "She is a friend of Barras."

"Citizen Director Barras?"

"He is, as you may know, my patron," said Talleyrand. "I am certain I can trust to your discretion when I tell you that I come to speak to you about this woman on his behalf."

"Yes, yes. Of course." The policeman began to straighten papers on his desk, as if expecting an inspection by Barras at any moment.

"He would consider it a personal favor if you were to release the file on this woman to me."

"A personal favor?"

"I am sure you can understand the need for a man as

important as the Director to learn all he can about his friends."

"Yes, yes. Of course," said the policeman.

Talleyrand left the police ministry with Catherine's file. He did no further work that day, but rather started home in his carriage, reading the police records on his house guest. There was nothing there to speak of. Yes, she had written letters to a deluded émigré, and she'd had some difficulties with her passport. But a year ago, a person could have gone to the guillotine for less.

Catherine's equipage was apparently in the carriage house, for his driver was able to bring him right to his front door. He was eager to see Catherine again, but there was a small part of him that regretted he could not have another first meeting with her. The encounter last night by the fire had been pure magic.

Auguste was there to take his cloak again. The servants were lighting lamps in the hallway against the gathering darkness of the street outside.

"Madame Grand asks if you will call on her in her room directly," said Auguste.

Talleyrand made his way to her room in the half light of a house attempting to rouse itself for its evening life. He scratched on the door.

"Come in, please," said Catherine's voice from behind the door.

He entered and found the room rather dark. He realized he was still holding Catherine's file. He could make out a form seated on a chair before the fire.

"Shall I call the servants to light the lamps?" he said.

"Don't bother," she said without turning around. The firelight glinted from her hair, which looked carefully arranged.

Talleyrand wondered how much of the day she'd had

to spend making her hair so elaborate. She was very much a lady.

"I prefer to remain here by the fire, Shortfoot. It's cold in here."

Talleyrand did not find it particularly cold.

He took several gliding steps around the chair to face her, and his breath caught in his throat. He had thought there was nothing she could possibly do to recapture the excitement of the previous night, but he was wrong. She sat in the chair before him and, while her posture was modest, she wore nothing but a dark velvet ribbon around her neck.

He tossed the file into the fire.

ELEVEN

PROTOCOL REQUIRED that the Minister of Foreign Affairs stand when addressing the assembled Directoire, so on damp days Talleyrand endeavored to keep his ministerial reports brief. Inclement weather made his lame leg hurt.

The high windows of the audience room at the Luxembourg Palace were streaked with raindrops. As Talleyrand was summarizing a petition received from the legislature of the Cisalpine Republic, a pain made him shift his weight to his good leg from the lame leg with its heavy brace. He looked up toward the low dais where the five men sat in their padded, thronelike chairs. Barras was staring toward the high ceiling in some sort of reverie. Reubell was picking a piece of lint from his breeches.

The other three Directors examined fingernails, fiddled with spectacles, scratched surreptitiously under jackets.

Talleyrand was tempted to say he had, on behalf of the Directoire, appointed a mission to the Man in the Moon, just to see what sort of reaction it might evoke. He suspected that there would be no reaction at all.

A distant roaring sound started up outside on the street, and the Directors all looked toward the windows.

"What is that?" said Barras.

"It sounds like cheering of some sort, Citizen Director," said Talleyrand.

"Cheering?"

Then the great double doors of the audience room opened behind him, and Talleyrand turned to see a soldier standing in the doorway.

"We are in a private audience. What is the meaning of this?" said Barras.

The soldier, who was a captain, was very young. He was covered with grime, and he needed a shave. There was a smudge on his cheek, and his blouse was torn at the shoulder. He held a mud-flecked dispatch case in one hand. In the other, he held a lance with some sort of banner furled around it.

"I bring the greetings of General Bonaparte," he shouted. Without waiting for an invitation, he strode toward the Directors' dais. The scabbard of his saber bounced against his hip, and his boots left mud on 'the parquet.

To a man, the Directors flinched in their chairs at the young man's approach, as if they thought he had come to announce a coup d'état.

Reubell recovered himself first. He was incensed. "Did the general instruct you to disrupt a closed meeting, captain?"

"The General sends news of imminent peace in

Europe!" The captain stopped at the edge of the dais and began unfurling his flag. "This is the captured standard of an Austrian battalion, destroyed by our forces at Lodi." The flag was apparently white at one time, but now it was beige, edged on two sides with gold fringe and on one side with the dark brown trim of incomplete burning. At its center, Talleyrand could make out the double-headed eagle of the House of Hapsburg. The young captain stood there holding his flag and smiling, as if to ask the Directors' opinion of it as drapery.

Talleyrand's good leg began to tire, and he shifted his weight to the brace, which dug into the flesh of his thigh and made him shift his weight back to the tired leg.

Barras gestured for a servant to take the flag from the captain. The captain beamed and handed it to the servant, who grasped the lance squeamishly and took it away.

"Milan is now open to the armies of the Republic." The captain brandished his dispatch case by its strap. "The Austrian army is outflanked, and Lombardy is ours."

Talleyrand shifted his weight to the brace again and gritted his teeth against the pain to give his good leg a rest. He could see that Reubell had not yet overcome his anger. A confrontation was going to unfold, and Talleyrand hated confrontation.

"Captain," said Talleyrand.

The young officer turned to face the foreign minister.

The roar outside grew louder.

"The Directors must continue their meeting, but please tell the General that they receive his news gratefully and wish him many more such victories. Please wait for a message to the General from the Foreign Ministry."

"Are you the foreign minister, citizen?" said the captain.

"At your service," said Talleyrand.

"Then I am to give this to you." The captain strode to

Talleyrand with his muddy dispatch case before him, dangling by its strap.

Talleyrand smiled and took the strap. He held the case aloft, as if in celebration of General Bonaparte's accomplishment, but more to keep it from rubbing against his freshly cleaned, wine-colored jacket.

"The General asked me to give you his compliments," said the captain.

Talleyrand could see the Directors watching him with suspicion. Their spies had apparently not told them their foreign minister was in regular communication with General Bonaparte.

"Thank you, captain. The Ministry secretary, downstairs, will find you a place to rest and clean up."

The captain bowed, turned, and walked toward the door. As he reached the door, Reubell shouted after him.

"Tell your general the people of France respect other republics, and he is to do nothing that would threaten Venice!"

The young captain turned to face them all.

"I will explain in my message," said Talleyrand.

The captain bowed, then stepped through the doorway and was gone.

"I do not need you to explain my commands," said Reubell.

Talleyrand wished Citizen Director Reubell had better manners, but then if he had, he probably would not have survived his government service. "It was a poor choice of words on my part, Citizen Director. I meant to say I would enjoin."

"Do you mock me, Citizen Minister?" The fire in Reubell's eye looked like it would burn the souls of the dozens he had sent to the guillotine.

Talleyrand put on the same face he used for whist and waited for the storm to pass.

"Let us resume your report, Citizen Minister," said Barras.

"We shall resume nothing!" Reubell wagged his fore-finger at Barras. "Bonaparte is going to destroy the Republic of Venice. He answers to no one on this Directoire, and it is your fault for visiting this Corsican pirate on us."

Barras, leaning back in his chair and with his hands resting on its arms, wore the aristocratic imperturbability for which he was known. "He answers with victories."

"Humph." Reubell, apparently without a suitable reply, turned to face Talleyrand.

Talleyrand shifted his weight to his brace again, then quickly back to his other leg when it pinched.

"Citizen Minister," demanded Reubell, "why are you dancing that way?"

Talleyrand shifted once more. "The Director may recall that I find it difficult to stand for long periods, as a result of a childhood injury." He looked around for a chair and, seeing one on the other side of the room, gestured for a servant to bring it.

"What are you doing, Citizen Minister?" said Reubell.

"He is going to sit down," said Barras. "He is lame."

"He'll sit down when I tell him to sit down," said Reubell.

The servant had started toward him with the chair, but Talleyrand waved him off.

"You're in league with this Corsican, and you're as much to blame as Barras for his behavior," said Reubell.

"To blame, Citizen Director?"

"That bandit is going to come to Paris and stage a coup against the legitimate government of the Republic."

Talleyrand did not think legitimacy counted for much when it was used as a shield for impotence, but he rarely spoke his thoughts aloud in the presence of his masters. "I will admit that the General is popular," he said, "but even the most popular of heroes can be turned to account."

"What do you mean?" Barras leaned forward in his chair.

"The General has secured his popularity partly with victories and partly with dramatic presentations," said Talleyrand. "The people may admire him for his victories, but they love him for the way he delivers his dispatches." He gestured toward the doorway through which the young captain had departed. As if in answer, the noise from the street intensified.

"That's true," said La Revellière, who always made a great show of despising any action that betrayed a lack of candor.

"I would suggest that the Directoire employ some drama of its own." Talleyrand's bad leg began to throb, but he did not let it show on his face. "The government should welcome the General home in a grand ceremony. Each of the Directors will wear his ceremonial regalia, and the General will be invited to present himself before the public. The comparison between the resplendence of the Directors in their robes of office and the plain appearance of the General in his uniform will magnify the popularity of the government and diminish the figure of the General."

One of the first official acts of the Directoire, when it was inaugurated two years before, had been to commission Jacques-Louis David, the laureate painter of the Revolution, to design the official robes of office for the government. Designed on the aesthetic principles of the classical republics, enhanced by the bright colors, lace, and ruffles of modern fashion, these costumes were more splendid than anything worn in Versailles at the court of the Sun King. There had not been a costume ball in France for nearly a decade, and Talleyrand knew the

Directors delighted in any opportunity to wear these outlandish outfits.

"What a grand idea!" said Barras. "We should not ex-
tinguish military glory, but we ought to illuminate it and
guide it." Barras was given to incomprehensible remarks.

"It could succeed," said Reubell sullenly.

"Citizen Minister," said Barras to Talleyrand, "please
plan the ceremony."

"It will be done," said Talleyrand.

Auguste was waiting for him among the inevitable
crowd of office-seekers and petitioners in the reception
room outside. The Minister and his servant walked together to the hallway beyond. It was not the first time
Talleyrand had left the Directoire with sore legs, and
Auguste knew what to do. As soon as they were out of
sight of everyone, he ducked under Talleyrand's out-
stretched arm and supported him on his weak side all the
way to the Minister's waiting carriage in the street.

🦁　　🦁　　🦁

As well as his official meetings with the assembled
Directoire, Talleyrand regularly met in private with
Barras to report on the work of his ministry and on any-
thing else that might be of interest to his patron.

"I feel I must apologize for Reubell, my friend," said
Barras.

"It is nothing, Citizen Director. Please do not worry
over it."

"Have you met with the mission from America?" said
Barras.

There had been disputes with the Americans over
shipping, and the United States had sent a delegation to
resolve matters with the French Government. Talleyrand
had been promising the Americans a meeting with Barras
for some months, but he was not prepared to arrange it

until they provided some token of their seriousness. The banker Gouveneur Morris was good for it. Talleyrand could not understand why they were taking so long to raise the money.

"The Americans say they would like a few more weeks to prepare their petition," said Talleyrand.

"They've already had a couple of months," said Barras. "I cannot understand these people. Tell me, do you think they are capable of providing us with some incentive to resolve the shipping dispute?"

"I doubt it, Citizen Director," said Talleyrand.

"Don't hurry their case, then," said Barras. "We have more pressing matters to deal with."

"As you wish, Citizen Director."

Barras pulled a sheet of paper from the drawer of his enormous desk, adroitly placed a pair of spectacles on the bridge of his nose, and began to read. "You may go."

Talleyrand struggled to his feet. "There is another small item of business, Citizen Director."

Barras looked up and gazed at Talleyrand over the spectacles.

"I have been to see the Minister of Police," said Talleyrand.

"Whatever for?"

"I thought the government may benefit from closer cooperation and communication among the heads of its various ministries."

"Good, good," said Barras.

"The Minister of Police expressed to me his desire to retire from government service and spend more time with his family."

"Then see to it," said Barras, and he went back to his document.

"One more thing, Citizen Minister."

"Yes?"

"The Minister of Police has served the government well under difficult circumstances. Perhaps the Treasury could provide him with a small grant to ease the burden of his retirement."

"Yes, of course," said Barras. "Excellent idea. Please take care of the presentation."

Talleyrand had no spring in his limping step when he left Barras's presence, but he might as well have. Not only had he rid himself of the policeman, but he had gained a cash payment into the bargain.

🦁   🦁   🦁

Talleyrand had been writing regularly to General Bonaparte, advising him on the political affairs of the Directoire and congratulating him on his many victories. The General's replies, dense with gratitude and eagerness to impress, bespoke a youthful idealism and confidence. Talleyrand knew that he must have suffered as much as anyone through the darker moments of the Revolution, but obviously believed in the greatness of France and the final triumph of civilization against the medieval forces of darkness. He never failed to reply to the foreign minister's letters, and he attended to their points in great detail.

Talleyrand had never met the young general, but he was impressed with the man's accomplishments, and he thought he might be just the kind of man the government needed to end the Directoire, which repeatedly demonstrated mastery of nothing other than recrimination, its preferred method for deliberating issues of national importance.

Citizen Director Reubell might be vexatious in his personality, but he had assessed the behavior of the General perfectly. Bonaparte, marching across the landscape of northern Italy, understood that the Directoire, for all its costumes and protocols, controlled nothing. And he an-

swered to no one on the Directoire. He answered, in fact,
to no one at all. As if to prove his independence to the
world, the General concluded his own peace with the
Austrians, and he did, in defiance of Citizen Director
Reubell's instructions, grant them title to Venice.

With the Treaty of Campo Fornio, which ended war on
the continent, the General returned to Paris.

Talleyrand heard from his friend Montrond that the
crowds of onlookers and admirers were so thick Bonaparte
had to take his own house in much the same way he had
taken the bridge at Lodi. Everyone wanted to get a look
at the man who had brought peace to Europe. He could
not walk down the street without a horde of people sur-
rounding him, and he was forced to take a small squad of
men with him on the humblest of errands, just to make
sure he was not crushed.

After reoccupying his house, the first place he paid
call was Talleyrand's home in the rue Taitbout.

Talleyrand came to the foyer to greet the General.
One could hardly do less for the prodigy who had, at the
age of twenty-eight, vanquished nearly all the enemies of
the Republic and subdued the greatest empire on the
continent.

A squad of lightly armed men in uniform entered
Talleyrand's foyer and stationed themselves along either
side of the room. Then the General entered. He wore
white breeches and a dark blue cutaway coat over a white
vest. The coat was decked with ribbons and devices on the
chest and surmounted with gold-fringed epaulets. He wore
a sword and carried under his arm a hat about the size of
a chaise. He was not a tall man, and his rigging appeared
to diminish his height even further.

The foreign minister limped forward and introduced
himself.

Bonaparte wore an expression Talleyrand could only

have described as "hurt." He wondered what the General might have seen with those deep yet piercing eyes that had marked him so.

The General stared unabashedly into Talleyrand's face, as if he hoped to discern whatever motives the foreign minister had hidden behind it. "I understand you are the nephew of the Archbishop of Rheims." He spoke with a marked Italian accent. "I have an uncle who is an archdeacon in Corsica. He raised me. In Corsica, an archdeacon is the same as a bishop in France, you know." He offered his hand.

Talleyrand took the hand. It was warm and dry. "Then we have a great deal in common, General."

Talleyrand had met the most interesting men in his forty-three years and thought he was no longer capable of being impressed by anyone. But this young conqueror of southern Europe, with his hurt expression and his touching desire to prove he was a gentleman, captured the Minister readily. He was short and pale and dressed in poor taste, but Talleyrand thought him handsome and reflected that twenty victories go very well with youth.

"I set great store by your observations and your advice," said the General, "and I want to thank you for your letters. They were the only communications I received from Paris that were of any use."

Talleyrand understood with surprise that the General was telling him openly that he had found the Directors, with their constant stream of orders and exhortations, to be a burden. It was plain the General would need some guidance about what he should say in public and when he should say it if he was going to survive in the environs of the treacherous Directoire.

"It is kind of you to praise my modest efforts," said Talleyrand.

Bonaparte looked around the foyer. "Is there a place we can talk privately?"

Talleyrand led the General to his office, and the two of them sat down to talk.

Amid all the General's more elaborate decorations, he wore a plain black ribbon, fastened around his upper arm.

Talleyrand assumed he was in mourning for a family member. "I am sorry for your loss, General."

Bonaparte looked down at the ribbon on his arm. "For all my losses," he said in a tone that sounded practiced. "In the brutal economy of the battlefield, one makes the expenditure of comrades. Sometimes for no better reason than to create a feint or assess the strength of an emplacement."

Talleyrand could not determine whether he was hearing the bravado of youth or the brutality of military will.

The General did not give him the opportunity to consider it further, however. He began immediately to unburden himself of his opinion of the Directoire. The General thought the Directors corrupt, incompetent, and venal. It was in spite of them that he had secured his many victories rather than as a result of their support.

"I am sure you needed very little help in gaining your victories," said Talleyrand.

"I do not trust any of those Directors," said Bonaparte. "Even Barras. I could tell from the tone of your letters that you don't trust them, either."

Talleyrand let this observation pass. He shifted himself in his chair. His leg was still hurting from the day before, when Citizen Director Reubell had again made him stand all afternoon.

"I have received a letter from the Directoire inviting me to be presented to them next week in a public ceremony in the Luxembourg's courtyard," said Bonaparte.

"I know," said Talleyrand. "I wrote it."

Bonaparte regarded him with his fine, piercing eyes for a moment. He did not speak. The clock on the mantle tocked away several seconds. Finally, he appeared to come to some sort of decision. "I am an excellent judge of men," he said. "I trust you, but I had assumed this ceremony was some kind of trick to make me look bad."

Talleyrand had not expected such directness, and he was at something of a loss as to how to handle it. Dissimulation he could handle, but candor and trust were outside his experience. As he regarded the General, he heard himself speak.

"The Directors expect to overawe you in the public's eye." Talleyrand had not intended to speak, and he realized with a start that the General's candor had somehow goaded him into an uncharacteristic directness of his own.

The General did not answer, but sat and stared at him.

This hurt-looking youth was a young man of unimaginable ferocity and strength. Talleyrand had read between the lines of the General's field dispatches, and he knew that his victories were the result of forced marches and a tolerance for heavy casualties.

Talleyrand thought about the clothes horses who sat on the Directoire, men whose primary qualification for public office was that they had survived the Terror. The General and the manipulators . . . they would never be able to live together. Was it better to be the friend of one who might make an "expenditure" of you on the field of battle or of one who would hold his tongue when you were dragged off to the guillotine?

One should choose the shrewdest, of course, but Talleyrand realized he himself was shrewder than any of them. It remained, then, to choose the one most likely to listen to him.

"I suggest that you seize the initiative and turn the Directors' ceremony around to your own advantage," said Talleyrand.

"Shall I bring a battalion?" said the General.

"No," said Talleyrand. "You should do just the opposite. Come alone. Do not even bring an aide-de-camp." Talleyrand looked at the decorations on the General's chest and the sparkling gold epaulets at his shoulder. "And do not wear a uniform. Dress yourself in civilian clothing, as plain as you can find. We shall present you to the people as a citizen soldier, who, having answered the call of his country, wants nothing more than to return to private life."

"But I don't want to return to private life," said the General. "Now that I have subdued the enemies of the Republic, I want to fulfill my destiny. I want to become a Director."

"The people of France are nervous, General," said Talleyrand. "They want to honor you, and they admire you, but in Paris every general is seen as a Cromwell."

Talleyrand knew the General possessed a good French education and would not fail to understand his allusion to the English dictator during that country's unfortunate Interregnum.

"People are wary," said Talleyrand. "If you really aspire to power, you must not seek it. If you will but put yourself in my hands, I will help you to navigate the government of the Directoire, for you are now in waters more treacherous than anything you have seen in battle."

The General regarded him silently. Then he studied the design in the carpeting for some moments, and Talleyrand wondered if he had made a mistake opening his heart to this young man. Finally, the General gestured for Talleyrand to proceed.

"The Directors intend to receive you in those outlandish costumes they wear for ceremonial occasions," said Talleyrand. "The comparison between the extravagance of the Directors in their robes of office and the modesty of the citizen soldier in his plain overcoat will capture the public imagination. The public is not happy with the Directoire, but they have had a succession of governments visited on them in the past nine years, and they do not want another change unless they are certain it will be for the better. Our goal over the next several weeks will be to persuade them that you are the best choice to lead us from this morass of incompetence. You have returned to Paris as a conqueror, General, but we shall present you to the people as a peacemaker."

Bonaparte nodded and gestured for Talleyrand to continue.

"It will be my duty," said Talleyrand, "to introduce you at this ceremony." Talleyrand thought of the farcical solemnity that would attend the ceremony — the prayers to Reason, the hymns to the Republic, the Directors posing as statesmen. He thought about the ridiculous costume he would have to wear as an officer of the Directoire. Oh, for a social occasion that would let people address one another as "Monsieur" and "Madame" and not have to worry about offending the sensibilities of the Jacobins.

Talleyrand looked again at the General. The young man could be more than a conqueror. He could be a deliverer.

"There's something else, General."

Bonaparte raised his eyebrows.

"I would like to give a grand ball, to be held at the Foreign Ministry."

Bonaparte smiled and his pale color reddened.

Talleyrand realized that the hero of Campo Fornio was blushing.

"No one has ever given a ball for me before," said the General.

"You deserve a hundred such balls, General," said Talleyrand, "but I don't think it will be appropriate for the ball to honor a citizen soldier. Let us proclaim it in honor of your wife."

The General regained his paleness, and Talleyrand thought he detected a hint of disappointment in his expression.

"Of course," said Bonaparte.

"I advise you to dress quite plainly for the ball as well."

Bonaparte nodded.

"In your letters and reports, General," said Talleyrand, "I could see that your strategy is always to put your opponent in the position of doing what you want him to do. That is what you must do now. By shunning all honors, you intensify the public's desire to honor you. It is the same principle employed in getting an enemy to chase you by feigning a retreat."

Bonaparte's eyebrows rose slightly, and Talleyrand could see that he understood the strategic analogy.

"When we finally give the public the opportunity to honor you properly, there will be no limit to what they are willing to give," said Talleyrand.

"One thing I have learned on the battlefield," said Bonaparte, "is that victory goes to the commander who applies the best men to the task at hand. In entrusting my reputation to your care, I feel I have chosen the best man."

"Only the most devoted, General."

🦁   🦁   🦁

The Directors suggested, with the force of a decree, that in planning the ceremony Talleyrand make use of the odious painter David.

David took on the assignment with enthusiasm. He placed the hallowed symbol of the Republic, the altar of

the nation, at one end of the courtyard. Behind the altar
he placed the other icons of the Republic, the statues of
Liberty, Equality, and Peace. Then he had gilded thrones
arranged for the Directors so that they faced the altar. He
insisted that the courtyard be draped with great banners
and draperies in the sacred red, blue, and white of the
Revolution.

The morning of the ceremony dawned in gloominess,
but the dignified courtyard of the Luxembourg looked
rather like a harlot in her undergarments.

The only concession Talleyrand had been able to wring
from the barbaric painter was the arrangement of the captured enemy standards. These David was content to leave
heaped in great piles at the wall opposite his carefully
arranged iconography, without any additional decoration
other than simple signs bearing the names of the
General's victories.

On the day of the ceremony, Talleyrand dressed in his
official ministerial costume. The main features of this costume were a cloak, breeches, and a coat, all in black. The
vest had the most frightful blue lapels, which were exceedingly ugly but nevertheless helpful in drawing the eye
away from the monstrous red lapels of the coat. Neither
the red lapels nor the blue lapels, however, was sufficient
to draw attention from the enormous white silk sash. The
collar, cuffs and laps of the coat exuded layers of multi-
colored embroidery. Where the outfit lacked ruffles, it sub-
stituted ribbons. Talleyrand was expected to wear this
stentorian panoply with a sword and cross-belt and a hat
to which were attached three brightly colored and very
large ostrich feathers.

He could not don this clothing without feeling like he
should be announcing the feats of an acrobatic troupe. It
would require all his skill to keep the ceremony for
General Bonaparte from becoming laughable.

At the Luxembourg, before the ceremony, Talleyrand

stood with General Bonaparte in a room overlooking the
courtyard. They gazed at the statues and tapestries as
citizens began to enter and seat themselves on the rising
benches built for the occasion on the street side of the
courtyard. An orchestra played republican songs, and
Talleyrand was pleased to see that people were looking
not at David's banners and the statues, but at the piles of
captured standards, which they pointed to and discussed
animatedly.

Not so General Bonaparte, who had apparently seen
enough of the captured standards. He appeared to be captivated by the hangings, altars, and statues.

"It is an offense against God to build an altar to the
nation," said the General. "But I think this ceremony will
be fitting recognition for one who is destined for greatness." He turned to look at Talleyrand.

Talleyrand, dressed as he was for a circus performance, envied the General his simple gray overcoat.

"I wish I could wear a suit like yours," said the
General.

Talleyrand realized that his plan denied the General a
quantity of pomp and ceremony that he might desire. He
remembered then just how young the General was, and he
wished it were prudent to give him what he wanted. But
he knew he must be firm. "Please believe me, General,
when I tell you that none of this silk and embroidery is a
match for the dignity you wear this morning."

They both looked back at the courtyard. The music
changed to a trumpet voluntary, and Citizen Director
Barras appeared at the entrance. He stepped slowly into
the courtyard, keeping time with the music. He wore a
red-and-gold cloak and a fantastic white collar which came
up to his ears. There was colored embroidery in the collar,
and the overall effect was to make it look as if his head
were the decoration on a large celebratory cake. Peeking

from beneath his cloak was a blue frock coat with gold braid and a short white jacket edged in gold. There was a long blue scarf tied about his waist, and a red cross-belt, and they were fringed in gold as well.

The country was plagued with shortages and loss, and Talleyrand wondered how the Directors could be so willing to tempt fate by parading themselves before the public in so much gold. He looked back at his young charge in the gray overcoat. "Come, General. It is soon time for our entrance."

When they arrived at the passageway to the court-yard, Talleyrand stood aside and gestured for Bonaparte to precede him. As he watched the gray overcoat move slowly into the gloom ahead of him, he was stung with a feeling of great tenderness. The young man carried himself so proudly; he seemed to shoulder the very future of France. He believed in the greatness of his country and the need to deliver it from its enemies and its many trials. Talleyrand understood how important it was to protect this young genius from being used by the Directoire.

As soon as Bonaparte emerged from the passageway into the courtyard, a shout went up from the crowd. It was so loud that it drowned out the music. In the tumult, Talleyrand could make out some of the cries.

"Long live Bonaparte!"

"Long live the Republic!"

The General acknowledged none of it and merely walked to the front of the altar as Talleyrand had instructed him to do. The crowd grew more excited, and some people began to throw flowers. The flowers had not come cheap at this time of year, but Talleyrand liked the effect and judged they were worth the money he had paid for them. Bonaparte stood defiantly in his plain overcoat as chrysanthemums and carnations struck the stone surface around him like cannon shells.

The cheering intensified. It was deafening.

Talleyrand decided to let it go on for a time before approaching the altar to deliver his address. It was clear the people would do anything this young man asked them to do. And Talleyrand felt that even he might be among them.

TWELVE

TALLEYRAND'S most difficult task was to keep Bonaparte occupied and out of the public eye. The people were ready to stage an orgy of ceremonies and celebrations for the General. And the General would have gloried in the attention. But the foreign minister knew he must keep public affection for his protégé bottled up until the key moment.

Talleyrand allowed the General to accept a membership in the National Institute and to confer on military matters with the Directoire, but otherwise he tried to keep him in seclusion. He limited Bonaparte's contact with political figures. He also suggested that Josephine, the young man's wife, dispense with the smart society people who had begun to collect around her.

The General was ill-suited to seclusion and chafed under Talleyrand's management of his affairs. Nevertheless, he seemed genuinely grateful to the older man for his help, especially for the ball Talleyrand had given in honor of Josephine.

"It was quite splendid," said the General. "Josephine says you have single-handedly restored French society."

"She is entirely too generous, General," said Talleyrand.

"Not at all," said Bonaparte sincerely. "She said Madame Grand is one of the most beautiful and graceful women she has ever met, and that it was wonderful to be among people who remember manners and civility."

"Madame Bonaparte is herself a rare beauty and is known throughout this country for her charity and the generosity of her spirit," said Talleyrand, "but I cannot disagree with her. Madame Grand is indeed a graceful woman."

The General smiled at Talleyrand's compliment to his wife, and the foreign minister thought it the first time he'd ever seen the serious-minded young man relax the tension in his jaw. Bonaparte, of course, had been the principal attraction at Josephine's ball and, dressed in his plain gray suit, he cut an imposing and unique figure for the young women in gauzy dresses who hung on his every remark and vied to catch his eye.

Talleyrand understood that the General had barely been an adult when the *ancien régime* was swept away, and he had grown up in Corsica in the household of a lawyer. He had no way of knowing what life had been like in Paris before the Jacobins. It made sense he would be susceptible to being dazzled by Talleyrand's meager attempt to recreate that life.

"You must count yourself very fortunate," said Bonaparte.

"Indeed," said Talleyrand, but he had lost the thread of the conversation.

"Any man would be proud to have a woman like Madame Grand," said Bonaparte.

"Yes, of course," said Talleyrand.

"I imagine there will be annulments and accommodations to work out," said the General, "but I promise you, friend, that when we have taken over this government, our reforms will make it possible for you to marry her."

"I am most grateful, General," said Talleyrand.

The General's remark preyed on Talleyrand's mind after that. He had never thought about marrying Catherine. She was, as Bonaparte said, a beautiful and graceful woman. And Talleyrand loved her passionate nature, for he found it afforded him frequent opportunities for getting away from the world, if only for an instant. But marriage? To what end? The General, he realized, was of a prudish turn of mind and had objections, as yet unvoiced, to Talleyrand's living with Catherine without the benefit of marriage.

He kept himself from dwelling on it, however. There was a government to be captured and a new leader to be groomed. And the leader often resisted the grooming.

General Bonaparte disliked idleness, and he disliked being outside the government. To provide him some occupation, Talleyrand persuaded the Directors to give him another command. Since France had but one enemy remaining, Bonaparte was appointed Commander in Chief of the Army of England.

Talleyrand watched as, with characteristic ferocity, the General threw himself into his preparations for an English invasion. Bonaparte impaneled a command staff, interviewed provisioners, and wrote pages and pages of plans. He kept an entire hall of clerks busy calculating costs. He toured barracks, inspected battalions, supervised drills, and attended artillery demonstrations. Then he left Paris for a month to inspect the forces that were assembling near Calais.

Talleyrand was grateful to have a month away from Bonaparte. He needed to re-establish several friendships that had fallen into disrepair as a result of his spending so much time looking after the General. So he called on

Madame de Staël, and he and Catherine played cards at the home of Madame de Flahaut. He called on everyone he had not seen since Josephine's ball.

It had been some time since Talleyrand had seen Montrond, and when he visited him he found his friend in a state of melancholy. Montrond's wife had run away in an apparent effort to humiliate her husband publicly. Talleyrand could see that Montrond needed to get out of his house, so he suggested a small dinner party in his own home.

"You know I would enjoy having dinner with you," said Montrond, "but I find it difficult to be with women these days, and I lack the stamina to endure the company of the thirty or forty people who are likely to be at your house."

Talleyrand could not understand why stamina might be required for a dinner party, but he could see Montrond was sincere.

"Then we shall have a dinner entirely of men," he said. "I will invite no more than six friends, well known to both of us, and we will have a quiet evening of male companionship."

Talleyrand could see he was dubious about the plan, but Montrond was too kind a man to do anything but agree.

Talleyrand invited the guests, but when he tried to explain the plan to Catherine, she would have none of it. She held Montrond in high regard for his role in bringing her together with Talleyrand, but she could not tolerate the idea that there might be amusement going on in the house outside her presence.

"I want to do something special for Monsieur de Montrond," she insisted.

Talleyrand was at a loss. He had come to understand that he could deny her nothing, but he had promised Montrond a dinner with only men. He finally agreed that

Catherine would be allowed to welcome the guests and to greet Montrond, but then she must withdraw.

On the evening of the dinner, Talleyrand's guests were all assembled, and yet Catherine had not appeared. Talleyrand was just beginning to feel impatient when Auguste entered the room and announced her. With her magnificent blond hair down well beyond her shoulders, Catherine walked into the room wearing nothing but a sparkling anklet and a black neck ribbon.

Talleyrand's six guests were stunned by Catherine's entrance. He himself endeavored never to be stunned by anything, but even he was overcome by her beauty and her audacity. He knew then that she was a precious jewel, and he must treasure her.

No one said a word as she walked up to Montrond and offered her hand. "Monsieur de Montrond, it is delightful to see you."

Talleyrand noticed that Montrond kept his gaze fixed firmly on her face as he said, "Seeing you, Madame Grand, is more enjoyable — and more stimulating — than a visit to the Louvre."

Catherine smiled and then went on to offer her hand to the other guests.

"My friend," said Talleyrand to Montrond, "you once did me a service, and I have not yet thanked you for it."

"At the time, I enjoyed doing it." Montrond looked at Catherine's smooth, round derrière as she greeted another guest. He looked like a farmer who had given away a colt and then learned it was an Arabian. "But now I find I can hardly tell the difference between charity and foolishness."

Catherine's presence seemed to improve Montrond's outlook markedly, so Talleyrand instructed one of the servants to set another place for her. For the rest of the evening, he tried to behave as if he were accustomed to hosting dinner parties in the company of a nude woman, and his guests struggled to follow his example.

Catherine sat between Talleyrand and Montrond, and Talleyrand could tell by the faces of the men opposite how often the movements of her head swept her hair aside to reveal her breasts. Talleyrand had never hosted a dinner with less talk, but the mood was convivial. Catherine's conversation — what there was of it — was more stimulating than he had ever known it to be, but he was not sure any of his guests noticed. Everyone except Talleyrand drank a great deal more wine than usual, and if there was not a great deal of talk, there was more than enough hilarity.

During the cheese and fruit, Talleyrand felt a presence near his elbow and looked up to find Auguste standing next to him.

The servant bent down and spoke in a soft voice. "General Bonaparte is here."

Talleyrand could not remember a time as an adult that he did not know what to do with a situation. It was a very strange feeling for him. He looked around the table at his laughing guests and the naked Catherine. He knew instinctively that his prudish general would react badly to this scene. Should he spirit Catherine away to her dressing room? Pull a curtain down from the window and wrap her in it? Send word that he was not at home? No course of action seemed to have anything to recommend itself. Fortunately, Auguste had already got the matter somewhat in hand.

"I have asked him to wait in the library, and I asked the cook to prepare a tray for him."

The calm, self-assured voice of his servant brought Talleyrand back to himself. Of course, he would entertain the General in the library. His guests did not even have to know the famous man was here.

He excused himself as gracefully as he' could and followed Auguste to the library.

He found the General seated before a plate on the reading desk with a white napkin tucked into the front of his collar. He had a fork in his left hand and a knife in his right and was dispatching a second game hen.

Bonaparte waved a greeting to him with the knife and then pointed it toward the chair opposite the desk.

"How delightful to see you, General." Talleyrand lowered himself into the indicated chair.

Bonaparte nodded and continue to chew. When he finished chewing and finally swallowed, he followed it with a great gulp of wine and then cut another bite of game hen, which he thrust into his mouth.

The situation was rather awkward but not unlike many that Talleyrand had endured during his visit to America. He sat and watched the General work his way through the game hen as if he were reducing an enemy redoubt one bite at a time.

The General finished eating, pushed aside the plate of small bones, and drained the rest of his wine glass. He pulled the napkin from his collar and wiped away the shine that had collected around his mouth.

"The time has come to turn these Directors out on the street." He sucked at his teeth, then dug between two of them with a fingernail. "I hear the most scandalous stories of their behavior. This city is infested with libertines and reprobates. They are sapping the moral fiber of this country. A handful of virtuous men will make short work of these characters."

Talleyrand thought it better to divert the General's thinking from the moral fiber of the country.

"Once you have conquered England, General," he said, "the country will be yours without a fight. No one will need to make short work of anyone else."

"Bah." Bonaparte looked impatient. "It is impossible. I cannot put an army at sea under the eyes of the English."

Talleyrand realized he had never before heard the General use the words "I" and "cannot" in the same sentence.

"It is a cliché that a general is doomed when he fails to understand his limitations," said Bonaparte. "But I say to you, my friend, that *my* greatest danger will come when I fail to understand my strength."

Talleyrand, whose education consisted chiefly of the study of the lives of bishops and saints, did not know enough military history to dispute this. "Go on, General."

"A battle is won," said Bonaparte, "by the general who applies the most powerful weapon — whether it be a regiment, a cannon, or a soldier with a bayonet — at the critical juncture. When you see that juncture, the strategy for winning is self-evident. I owe my victories to having always chosen the time and place for this juncture to occur. And that juncture is not at sea under the eyes of the English. As contemptible as they are, they are good with ships."

Talleyrand found this small measure of self-doubt refreshing.

"Is there anywhere else to meet them?" he said.

"Not that I can see. We have driven them from the continent. They have nothing here we can threaten; I see no way to draw their attention."

"What about a different continent?" said Talleyrand.

The General looked thoughtful. "India," he said at last. Then he added, almost too softly to be heard, "Alexander went to India."

Talleyrand rather liked the idea of having the General off marching around on a different continent.

"But not a direct assault," said Bonaparte. "We should seize their supply routes first."

"Egypt?" said Talleyrand.

But before the General could answer, the library door opened, and sounds swept into the room from the hallway, just ahead of a gale of laughter from the dining room.

Both men looked toward the doorway. Catherine stood there in her anklet and neck ribbon.

Talleyrand sensed the General tensing in his chair and realized Catherine had just earned them classification among the libertines and reprobates who were sapping the moral fiber of the country.

"General," she said, "how delightful to see you!"

She advanced into the room, and Bonaparte, speechless, said nothing.

Talleyrand stood. "Is dinner finished, my dear?"

"The men are having tobacco and brandy." She extended her hand across the desk to Bonaparte.

Bonaparte stood. He kissed Catherine's hand stiffly, then looked at Talleyrand as if trying to comprehend what was happening.

"My dear," said Talleyrand, "the General and I are engaged. Would you excuse us?"

"Oh, pooh." She sighed. "I suppose I will retire. General, please remember me to Madame Bonaparte."

The General said nothing, but Catherine appeared not to notice that he had not spoken since she entered the room. She smiled fetchingly at Talleyrand, then left. When she closed the door, the room became quiet as a tomb.

The two men sat down again. Talleyrand decided he must break the silence.

"The Republic of Virtue is gone, General. Some of the more spirited of our citizens seem to feel they have been bottled up too long."

Napoleon nodded and stared at Talleyrand for several moments. Finally he spoke.

"I believed when I married Josephine that she was a wealthy member of the old aristocracy. I still love her, but

I discovered that was not the case. She was the impover-
ished daughter of colonials, and she happened to marry
an aristocrat who became a revolutionary during the
Terror. She lost everything when he went to the guillotine."

Talleyrand wondered what he was getting at.

"She was never a real aristocrat," said Bonaparte.
"You, my friend, are my only link to the aristocracy of the
old world. If we are to restore order and civilization to
France, we must be able to recreate the old ways. Tell
me, did women of the nobility undress themselves at dinner parties in those days?"

"It may have happened from time to time," said
Talleyrand. "But I don't think it was the rule."

"It should not become so then," said Bonaparte.
"Please tell Madame Grand to wear clothing to dinner
from now on."

"Of course," said Talleyrand.

"And once we have taken control of the government,"
said the General, "you will marry her."

In April, at Talleyrand's suggestion, the Directoire
appointed Bonaparte Commander of the Army of the East,
and in May the General left Paris with his expedition. In
June he conquered Malta. In July he landed at Alexandria
and deployed the French army in Egypt. Paris was electri-
fied with his dramatic dispatches describing battles in a
far-off land under the sight of the pyramids, but
Talleyrand wondered what trials and tribulations these
dispatches concealed about an army with no desert experience.

Talleyrand thought the conquest of Egypt an excellent
plan, however, for it removed the unifying presence of the
General and allowed the politics of France to grow uglier

every day. And it occupied the General thoroughly without disturbing the peace of Europe. Why set armies marching across Europe when there were foreign lands to absorb their energies?

The peasants of the Vendée once again hoisted the Bourbon standard and attacked the republican troops. In the National Assembly, there were calls for re-erecting the guillotine in the Place de la Révolution.

The situation looked increasingly difficult as the annual drawing drew near. In May of each year, according to the rules, one of the five Directors — whose name was chosen by lot — vacated his seat. Talleyrand spoke privately with four of the Directors, pointing out to each one how much more secure his seat would be if all five tokens in the lot bore the name of Citizen Director Reubell. They were not hard to convince. In response to a poll that Talleyrand took by going from office to office, the Directors voted to put the foreign minister in charge of the lot drawing. Talleyrand stopped his poll after the fourth vote. With that many votes in favor of his plan, it did not seem necessary to secure Reubell's vote in the matter.

Talleyrand made a public ceremony of the drawing, even though it meant wearing his hated uniform. He wanted to have lots of people there to see and thereby help to prevent anything untoward resulting from it. When a child pulled a token from the jar and read the name of Reubell, the chosen Director could not object unless he wanted to appear indecorous and a possible usurper. With the agreement of the other Directors, Talleyrand met with him after the ceremony to provide him with enough cash to get him to go quietly.

When the Director arrived at Talleyrand's office, Talleyrand rose from his desk to greet him.

"Please sit down, Citizen Director."

The foreign minister realized there was nothing to be gained by making Reubell stand.

Both men sat down.

"On behalf of the entire Directoire," said Talleyrand, "I would like to wish you well and to commend your unselfish service to the Republic."

"Let's not waste time, you scoundrel," said Reubell.

Talleyrand was shocked at the man's speech, but betrayed none of it in his face.

"How much will you give me to give up my seat without raising the alarm over this rigged drawing?"

Talleyrand knew he could prove nothing about the drawing, but he also knew Reubell could raise havoc in the Assembly and perhaps a riot in the streets. "Five thousand."

The Directoire had authorized ten thousand.

Reubell glared at him. "Don't insult me. Make it fifteen."

The bargaining went on for much of the remaining afternoon, and Talleyrand found the Director to be as shrewd as he was crude. In the end, he agreed to nine thousand, and felt certain that he had gotten Reubell as low as he could get him. It was unfortunate, for it left him with only one thousand for his efforts, which hardly seemed adequate for the service he had performed in getting rid of the man. Perhaps he could make up some of the deficit on the Americans.

Then again, sometimes the achievement itself is the reward. No longer would the foreign minister have to stand before the Directors for hours at a time.

It was time, of course, to elect Reubell's successor. One by one, Talleyrand met with the principal members of the National Assembly. He called in favors, he persuaded, he demonstrated logic, he made promises. He suggested to every member that the greatest problem faced by the country was neither resurgent revolution nor

counter-revolution. The greatest problem was factionalism
and civil war, and the only way to reduce factionalism was
to elect a moderate candidate to the Directoire. Fortunately,
Talleyrand knew such a candidate, and he advanced the
cause of Emmanuel Siéyès, a former priest with whom
Talleyrand had served in the Second Estate back in what
now seemed an ancient time.

Each of the four Directors advanced the cause of his
own particular candidate as well, but in the end the
National Assembly chose Siéyès, moderation, and
compromise.

Talleyrand called on Siéyès as soon as his friend's
election was confirmed. He found him being fitted for his
Directorial circus suit. Siéyès stood with a straight back
in a blue frock coat that had not yet been embellished
with gold braid and piping. The sleeves were on his arms
but unattached at the shoulders, and a tailor with a
mouth full of pins fussed around his back with a measur-
ing tape and a piece of chalk.

"Welcome, Citizen," he said to Talleyrand.

"Please accept my congratulations on your election,
Citizen Director," said Talleyrand. "The Directoire is fortunate to acquire a voice for moderation in troubled times."

"What news of your General?" said Siéyès.

"The General has taken Cairo and has promised the
Egyptian people liberation from their Mameluke oppres-
sors," said Talleyrand.

Talleyrand made his remarks for the benefit of the
tailor. Both he and Siéyès knew that Bonaparte's fleet
had been destroyed at Aboukir and the Egyptian armies
had consistently eluded the French. But in a world in
which one could not always tell who was working on behalf of the Bourbons and who on behalf of the radicals, it
was dangerous to voice discouragement.

Siéyès dismissed the tailor, and the two men sat down at a small table on the side of the room to speak frankly.

"Russia and Turkey have declared war on France," said Talleyrand.

Siéyès nodded. "This will give comfort to the royalists. They prosper these days because the revolutionaries are in disarray. Our government is a sinkhole of corruption, and the only people who uphold the principles of the Revolution want to do it with the guillotine."

Talleyrand never put much faith in the principles of the Revolution, or in any other principles for that matter. And he had always thought the guillotine a rather heavy-handed instrument of government.

"What we need is one strong man to sweep away the politicians and make honest, competent government," said Siéyès.

"I could not agree more," said Talleyrand.

Siéyès looked down at his blue frock coat. He pulled one of the unattached sleeves from his arm and tossed it on the table. "When does your general return?"

"As soon as he knows he has your support," said Talleyrand.

Siéyès, as if ridding himself of his obligations to the corrupt sinkhole that was Revolutionary government, pulled the other coat sleeve off and threw it on the table. "Tell him I would be interested in speaking with him."

🦁   🦁   🦁

Talleyrand did not know what awakened him. He clutched at the memory of a delicious oblivion even as he understood that he was lying in bed, awake and wondering where his sleep had gone. He could hear Catherine snoring softly beside him. When he looked up into the gloom, he saw someone was standing over him. Was he to be assassinated? But the figure spoke, and it was Auguste.

"I brought no candle, as I did not wish to wake Madame Grand."

"Thank you," whispered Talleyrand.

"General Bonaparte is here to see you."

Auguste had already found his dressing gown. He held it up while Talleyrand slid his arms into the sleeves, then picked up the leg brace from the floor beside the bed and helped his master limp to the hallway.

A few minutes later found Talleyrand, feeling both sleep-ridden and curious, entering the sitting room where Auguste had placed the General. The room was lit by a newly laid fire. The General paced the floor. When the door closed with a click behind Talleyrand, the General stopped and turned toward him with characteristic intensity. The foreign minister thought at first that his protégé did not know him. But, then, who could know him in his dressing gown and with his hair unpowdered? The General seemed to take it all in, however, and advanced on him as decisively as if he were at the head of a battalion.

"My friend." He grasped Talleyrand and kissed him on either cheek.

Talleyrand smelled the road dust on him, and he was flattered the General would come directly to see him. He was apparently forgiven the incident of Catherine's nudity. He was not surprised. Moral qualms rarely survive political necessity. It was one of the rules that allow human beings to live together on Earth.

"It is good to see you, General." Talleyrand led him toward the fire, where there was a well-padded chair and a sofa.

The two men sat down.

"I wish I had known when you were coming, General," said Talleyrand. "Now is the time for you to be seen and celebrated by the people. I could have arranged a triumphal march for you and your troops."

"I have no troops," said the General. "The army remains in Egypt under the command of General Kléber."

The General did not seem particularly concerned about the army he had left behind, and Talleyrand realized that one must cultivate a certain coldness of heart if one is regularly required to spend the lives of others in battle.

"In what state have you left that country, General?"

"I have given those poor bastards civilization," said the General, "if they can keep it."

Talleyrand had supposed that those poor bastards had civilization thirty-five centuries before the French acquired it.

"Paris is buzzing with news of your exploits," said Talleyrand. "You are the man of the hour."

"Good," said Bonaparte. "I think it is time I became a Director."

"General," said Talleyrand, "the Directoire is doomed. The people of France will be happy with nothing less than a whole new government, a whole new constitution. They want a strong leader who will sweep away the rats' nests and give them peace and justice."

Bonaparte's eyes shone in the firelight. "Peace and justice," he said. Then he spoke quietly, so that Talley-rand had to strain to hear him. "Augustus brought the people peace and justice."

Talleyrand thought it rather endearing that the General — scion of a petit bourgeois family — should aspire to compare himself with the principal member of the noblest family in history.

"I have spoken to Citizen Director Siéyès," said Talleyrand. "He believes that you will help him to take control of the government and make way for him to lead the country."

"But *I* intend to lead the country," said the General.

"And so you shall," said Talleyrand. "The best way to
be assured of his cooperation is to allow him to think he
is directing affairs."

"Is there a way to do this?"

"Soon he will approach you," said Talleyrand. "He
needs a general to fulfill his plans. Joubert is dead.
Bernadotte is too much a Jacobin, and Moreau will never
do it. You are his only choice. When he approaches you,
you must say that you will support him, but only in the
formation of a provisional government, pending the writing of a new constitution."

"Will he accept this?"

"As I have said," said Talleyrand, "he has no choice."

"Shall we then put the members of the National
Assembly on trial?"

"We need them to ratify a new constitution," said
Talleyrand. "If we plan all of this well enough, there will
be no need for trials or recriminations or musketry. We
will design a government in which you and Monsieur
Siéyès hold the highest offices. But it is your heroism and
leadership that has captured the public imagination, and
you will naturally become the head of the government. It
simply requires a cool head — which you have proved
many times that you possess — and patience, which you
must yet learn."

The General nodded, apparently willing to defer to
anything the older man said.

"Here is the plan I will put before Siéyès," said
Talleyrand. "The Directors will all resign simultaneously
in the face of the current public disorders."

"But why would they all resign?" said the General.

"I shall talk with each of them about the matter," said
Talleyrand. "We can offer them cash settlements from the
public treasury if necessary."

The General frowned but gestured for Talleyrand to continue.

"The Council of Elders will declare a state of emergency and give you command of the troops in Paris. Your troops will then protect the National Assembly while it votes the new government into existence."

The General listened intently as Talleyrand explained the plan, nodding occasionally to show that he understood. The foreign minister could see in the General's eyes that he was beginning to imagine himself executing the plan, that he was even now living out the movements, the speeches, the troop formations, the orders . . . all at the speed of thought. It was Talleyrand's experience that such a mental rehearsal was the mark of a man who controls events and bends them to his will. It was an ability foreign to Talleyrand. Not that he was lacking in imagination, but there was something inside him that said if he had already experienced the execution of a plan, even in his head, then there was little point in going through with it.

As he saw the General taking in the details of who should be bribed, who sent away, who commended, and who named to various positions, he wondered if the General counted the dead when he rehearsed a battle plan — if he saw the severed limbs and the bloody faces, heard the cries, smelled the gore.

He finished his recitation and watched the General for a reaction.

The General nodded again, then spoke.

"Do you know where you might purchase a château of considerable grandeur?" he said.

Talleyrand was taken aback. Why should the General be thinking of châteaux at a time like this? "There is a property in Valençay," he said, "one hundred eighty kilometers from here. The owner is from a very old family and under suspicion. He would be happy to let the château go at·a reduced price in return for the promise of official acceptance."

"Good," said the General. "I want you to make the promise and buy the property for yourself. Just make it available for entertaining dignitaries and heads of state in a grand manner. I know I can trust you to show important visitors how gracious and civilized France is under the new government. I think it is fitting that it be your house, for you are our link to the glories of the *ancien* days."

"Of course, General." Talleyrand felt his chest suffuse with warmth. He was going to have the chance to recreate his grandmother's style of living. Chalais would be reborn at Valençay. "I will be honored."

🦁   🦁   🦁

It took weeks to prepare for the coup. The conspirators — Siéyès, Bonaparte, and Talleyrand — met often to discuss arrangements. Bonaparte was in charge of the army, Siéyès was in charge of public affairs, and Talleyrand was given responsibility for managing the Directoire, which meant keeping its members in the dark.

Because so much of the planning took place at the Luxembourg Palace, where Citizen Director Barras lived, it was nearly impossible to exclude the most powerful man in the government. Talleyrand suggested that they bring Barras into the plan, at least until it was completed. Everyone agreed. When Talleyrand suggested to his patron that there was a well-organized plan to overthrow the government, Barras joined in the plot enthusiastically.

Talleyrand began to meet with Barras daily to explain to him how affairs were proceeding. He made up plans and details to share with Barras, but he kept them fairly close to what the conspiracy was actually planning in order to make it easier to avoid being caught in a lie — not that there was any real danger, for in their conversations Barras never questioned anything that mattered. He seemed more concerned with the official robes and the titles of the new government than with its policies or structure.

"I am in close contact with the most influential men in the Assembly," said Talleyrand on one occasion. "On the appointed day, they will vote you, General Bonaparte, and Citizen Director Siéyès as Consuls for life."

"Consuls?" said Barras. "Like the Roman Consuls?"

"Yes," said Talleyrand. "The classical allusion is rather nice, don't you think?"

"But inaccurate," said Barras. "There were only two Consuls in the Roman Republic. There are three of us."

"I doubt if the citizenry will be repairing to their history books to count Consuls," said Talleyrand.

"Of course," said Barras. "Please keep me informed as the plans progress."

After such a meeting, Talleyrand would report back to General Bonaparte and Citizen Director Siéyès on the meeting, while Citizen Director Barras went back to his primary occupation, which was the entertainment of dancing girls in a private apartment of the Luxembourg.

When the day neared for the execution of the plan, Siéyès and the General agreed that it should be Talleyrand who would meet with Barras. While the army was securing the National Assembly, Talleyrand would explain to him how affairs actually stood and persuade him to retire in the face of events he was powerless to resist. The other conspirators agreed to pay Barras one hundred thousand from the public treasury. The payment was suggested by Talleyrand, who was anxious that the change in government be unique in the annals of history — a polite coup d'état.

And so, the afternoon before the National Assembly was scheduled — under the protection of army bayonets — to vote emergency powers to Siéyès and the General, Talleryand went to see Barras with a letter of resignation and a letter of credit providing one hundred thousand for the bearer.

The dancing girl entertainments had not yet begun, and Barras received Talleyrand in his grand, sunny office with the monumental desk.

"How is the plan proceeding?" said Barras.

"Very well." Talleyrand removed the letter of resignation from his portfolio and laid it face down on the desk. "The Assembly will vote on emergency powers for the Consuls tomorrow."

"Do you think I should remain here during the voting?" said Barras.

"No, Citizen Director. I think you should be out of the city."

"Out of the city?" said Barras. "I don't understand. How can I assume my new office if I am not in Paris?"

"Consul Bonaparte and Consul Siéyès have asked me to apologize to you on their behalf," said Talleyrand.

Barras's face hardened into stone.

"I should have expected this," said Barras.

"I believe you did, Citizen Director," said Talleyrand. "You mentioned to me that the Roman Republic had only two Consuls."

"What do you intend to do with those who oppose you?" said Barras.

"I hope there will be no opposition," said Talleyrand. "But if there is, the army is loyal to General Bonaparte, and it has broad experience with firing squads."

Talleyrand could see the fear in Barras's eyes, and he shifted uncomfortably in the chair. Important work, especially political work, always involved unpleasantness.

"You can write your memoirs," said Talleyrand. "You have had an extraordinary vantage point from which to watch the most remarkable period of French history."

"I suppose I am fortunate not to be shot," said Barras.

"We knew it would not be necessary," said Talleyrand. "And we were all pleased about that. The others love you as much as I do."

Barras had the look of a man who had suffered a snake bite, and Talleyrand wondered why he should be so bitter. He'd had his day in the sun. He had survived the Terror, wielded substantial power, and entertained dancing girls. But more important, he had amassed a substantial fortune. He could live in sybaritic comfort for the rest of his life. He picked up the letter of resignation and turned it over on the desk.

"We expect to do this peacefully, but it is always possible there could be trouble," said Talleyrand. "The sooner you sign, the sooner you can take yourself safely to your château."

Barras nodded. He took a pen from the holder on his desk, pulled the letter over to him, and signed it without reading it.

Talleyrand stood up and reached over to take the letter. He had to stand holding it for a moment while the ink dried on Barras's signature. It was an awkward moment, and Talleyrand disliked awkward moments. But he thought about the letter of credit in his portfolio, the one that promised an unspecified bearer one hundred thousand, and decided that such a sum was worth a certain amount of awkwardness.

PRINCE

THIRTEEN

I LOOK AROUND, and I see mostly darkness. My duchesse Dorothée sits on a chair by my bed. Her hands move quickly over a piece of cloth stretched like a drum head on a circular frame. Pauline and her confessor speak in low, quiet tones on the other side of the room. I can hear them quite clearly.

"Sunrise will come in a few hours."

"Do you think it will rain again today?"

They are seated around my deathbed, but all have begun to resume their own lives. I am the only one who remains focused on my death. I am uncertain whether I should be pleased to see signs of normality around me. I know that for the living life must go on, and life requires needlepoint and chatting about the weather.

But they *must* understand that this is not someone else dying. It is I. I will be gone. My death should leave a hole in their world.

I once heard a man from the east say that we are all waves and life is an ocean, and we do not die but are simply dissipated in order to become part of the next wave. It sounds poetic and profound, and I suppose it would offer comfort to a more imaginative man in his final hours. But I have never been comforted by the profound. I would rather think shallow thoughts and live a little longer.

But that is not to be. I must think profoundly now, for soon I will not be thinking at all.

I will break on the beach alone, and the others will

finish their needlepoint and study the sky for signs of rain.

I block out their words, but I continue to watch Father Dupanloup and Pauline talk. They are so young. Pauline does not know what it meant to live in the days before the Revolution. Perhaps I am the last one who does.

Father Dupanloup's gaze drifts around the room and stops on my face, and he sees that I am looking at them. He rises and walks over to the bedside, still wearing his vestments.

The others join him, and the three of them are gathered round me now. They look at me expectantly, and it is plain that none of them thinks I will last very much longer. And the concern in their faces momentarily convinces me. Fear clutches at my chest like an undersea creature dragging me to the depths. This fear is monstrous, and yet there is a small voice that tells me it is only fear and nothing more. It is not yet time. I will continue a while longer. It could be days yet. Days of this? Can I bear it?

Pauline begins to weep, and the tears drop on my bedclothes. Dorothée's eyes sparkle with tears not yet spilled out onto her face.

I am sorry that my dying has interrupted their pursuit of normalcy. They must be tired of this. They must be strongly tempted to tell me to just get on with it.

But they will not, for they know there is business to be transacted before that.

Dorothée leans down, puts her arm around Pauline, and gently pulls her back away from my bedside. Then she takes her place there. She leans over and presses her hand to my forehead again.

"Won't you please sign it now?"

I want to sign it. I want whatever comfort my signing

will provide us all. But I think about the Pope's dissatisfaction with such a meager apologia from the greatest sinner of the century. I think about the monsignor turning away my family. His Holiness has refused the recantation. The sinner's body cannot be interred in consecrated ground.

My only chance of getting into that cemetery is to be under the ground before the Pope can read the recantation. I must make certain that signing is my final act. I must endure this for a time yet.

"No."

Fourteen

TALLEYRAND WAS NOT a traveler. In his visits to England and America in the waning years of the eighteenth century, he had as much traveling as he ever hoped to do. He found no enjoyment in bouncing coaches, endless mud, or uncertain meals.

But in the budding years of the nineteenth century, he found himself in the service of a man — Napoleon I, Emperor of the French — who was determined to bring the benefits of French civilization to the rest of Europe. The Emperor did not seem to mind that bringing the benefits of French civilization to other countries meant conquering them first. In fact, he apparently liked that part of the process best. So his gift giving required that he charge about the continent in the vanguard of the Grand Army.

And he left in his wake toppled dynasties, disintegrat-

ing social orders, and angry, vanquished opponents, all of
which had to be cleaned up and put to rights via treaties
negotiated by his foreign minister.

So Talleyrand bounced in coaches, surveyed endless
mud, and ate uncertain meals, trailing after the Emperor's
army like a camp follower. No sooner had one treaty been
executed and dispatched to Paris and the care of his deputy foreign minister, Reinhardt, than it was time to draw
up another. He was glad he had Reinhardt to hold things
together back home, and he longed for the day he could
join him.

The Austrian countryside in December 1805 was particularly bleak. Not only was the weather wet, gray, and
cold, but the people were beaten. There were burned-out
farms across the landscape, soldiers wounded and in rags,
townspeople hiding. News of the Emperor's glorious
victory at Austerlitz may have been inspiring delirious joy
back in Paris, but here it simply added to the misery of
people who woke up to find armies tearing up their fields
and clogging their highways.

The foreign minister had been a three days' coach ride
behind the Emperor when he got word of the victory at
Austerlitz. And with the news came an imperial order
that Talleyrand should join his sovereign at a house be-
longing to the prince von Kaunitz. This, he decided, was
an opportunity to persuade the Emperor to stop waging
war and, incidentally, to let his foreign minister go home
to Paris.

Talleyrand climbed into his coach and endured as
miserable a ride as he had ever had through the mud of
the battle-scarred Austrian roads to join his Emperor.
When he was still a day from the Emperor's headquarters, his coach was delayed for several hours by an artillery piece stuck in the muddy road. Four French soldiers
were supervising a group of miserable-looking Austrian

prisoners, who stood knee-deep in their tattered uniforms futilely trying to turn the spokes of the gun's wheels.

Talleyrand watched the fiasco from his coach. The French soldiers strode back and forth shouting and screaming at the prisoners, who seemed rather reluctant to receive these particular benefits of French civilization. As he watched, Talleyrand saw one of the French soldiers strike a prisoner with his rifle butt, knocking him face down into the mud. He was tempted to point out to the man that this was unlikely to improve the prisoner's performance, but he never interfered in military affairs.

It occurred to him that the rifle clubbing he witnessed was something of a metaphor for the Empire's behavior in Europe. He was lost in this thought when he heard a banging on his coach door.

"Please, sir!"

The door opened, and a bedraggled woman stood there. Her clothing was torn, and her face was covered with grime.

"Have you any— "

She was interrupted by a soldier who yanked her away and pushed her aside.

"Sorry, Your Excellency," he said. "These people aren't getting much to eat, and sometimes they get out of control."

"That's all right," said Talleyrand. "I understand."

The soldier began to close the coach door.

"Wait," said Talleyrand.

"Excellency?"

He took a coin from his pocket and tossed it to the soldier. "Give her that. Perhaps she can buy something to eat."

The soldier caught the coin neatly. "It's not likely, Excellency. There's nothing around here to buy."

"Give it to her anyway," said Talleyrand.

The obstacle was cleared shortly, and he was on his way again.

The prince von Kaunitz was not at home when Talleyrand arrived, which was to be expected. He was among the vanquished out in the countryside somewhere. Appropriating his house was one of the simple gestures the Emperor was so fond of using to show his beaten opponents that they were truly beaten. An aide-de-camp met the foreign minister at the entrance to the palace, escorted him to the Emperor, then left the two men alone.

The hero of Marengo sat at his dining table in the unadorned uniform of a colonel, which he still preferred, though he would have been entitled to wear ermine had he been of a mind to. To the Emperor's credit, however, despite his predilection for costume, he never dressed the imperial part except for ceremonial occasions. And he never induced the National Assembly to award him titles or honors the way monarchs had done since the days of Augustus. But then, Talleyrand supposed Emperor of the French was title enough for any man.

"You must join me in this," said the Emperor. "It is called chicken marengo. It will be excellent. I told the cook I would deport him to America if it is anything less."

"I am certain it will be delicious, Your Majesty." Talleyrand leaned against his cane. He decided he did not particularly want to eat with the man responsible for all this destruction. "But I am engaged for dinner this evening, and I eat but one meal a day."

"Suit yourself." The Emperor stabbed at the chicken with his fork and sawed a chunk from it with his knife. He popped the chunk into his mouth and watched Talleyrand as he chewed. He did not invite his foreign minister to sit down. But Talleyrand was used to standing in Napoleon's presence, at least since the coronation, which was about the time the Emperor had stopped inviting people to sit.

Talleyrand had learned that it was best to raise his own business first if he wanted it discussed at all.

"Sire," he said, "Your Majesty has enjoyed a triumphal entry into Vienna. He has utterly reduced the largest nation on this continent."

"It is good," said the Emperor. "The mushrooms are tender, and the onions are really quite sweet."

When Talleyrand saw how pleased the Emperor was with chicken marengo, he thought it might be a useful element in his program. "Generations hence, Your Majesty, people will remember the imperial genius when they eat this dish, as well they might. France is master of a continent, and there is no major power left to oppose her Emperor."

The Emperor said nothing, but — although he never risked the indignity of a smile — it was plain he agreed with the sentiments. He took a sip of wine from a gold goblet with the eagle crest of the Austrian Hapsburgs on it.

"But I beg Your Majesty to proceed with deliberation," said Talleyrand. "The Austrians will be more useful as allies than as enemies."

"The Austrians," said the Emperor, "are useful to no one, not even themselves." He took another bite of his chicken.

"It is true," said Talleyrand, "that the Austrian monarchy is an ungainly amalgamation of disparate countries and now incapable of posing a military threat, but she is an adequate buffer against the barbarians, and she is a necessary one. France may be opposed by no major power, but hordes of small tribes can menace us, as they did the Caesars."

Napoleon swallowed the bite he was chewing, and he

looked as if he were listening more intently. The word
Caesar always seemed to get his attention.

"Today, Austria is crushed and humiliated," said
Talleyrand, "and she needs her conqueror to extend a
friendly hand to her, to make her an ally and restore the
confidence she has lately lost. She will never again be
strong enough to be a threat to France. If Your Majesty
acts wisely now, she can nevertheless be an asset to him.
Your Majesty has the opportunity to be Europe's peacemaker."

The Emperor regarded him silently. He took another
sip of wine, then looked off in the distance. Finally he
turned back to Talleyrand and spoke. "You are forgetting
something."

"Sire?"

"You have offered me the opportunity to be Europe's
peacemaker many times since I met you. I have no ambi-
tion in that direction. I did not come into this world to
make peace. I came here to fulfill my destiny. I suspect
you are the one who wants to be Europe's peacemaker."

The remark arrested Talleyrand's thinking for a
moment. Was that true? Did he want to be Europe's
peacemaker? He had always worked for peace, but he had
always supposed he did so simply to avoid having to look
out his coach window and see wounded people and plun-
dered property. It would be a question to ponder at some
point. For now, he knew the discussion was slipping out
of his grasp. The Emperor had mentioned his destiny.
That was usually a reliable signal that he was tired of
talking about anything anyone else wanted to discuss and
was anxious to talk about things that mattered more to
him.

Talleyrand decided there might be room in the
Emperor's mind to hear one last appeal.

"Your Majesty," he said, "France will always be

stronger surrounded by friends than surrounded by enemies."

"But I was surrounded by enemies," said the Emperor, as if he and France were one and the same, "until I conquered them. I have no need of friendship. I only need obedience, and I wish the Austrians to understand this." He took another bite of chicken marengo and chewed it with obvious enjoyment, as if reliving the battle for which it was named.

Finally he spoke again. "I want you to negotiate terms with the Austrians that are advantageous to me."

Talleyrand could see that in the contest between sanity and the Emperor's destiny, destiny had won the field, at least for this engagement. There was nothing he could do now except hope for an opportunity to influence the Emperor later. He nodded his assent.

The Emperor began to give instructions, watching Talleyrand's face as he did so, as if after all these years he still thought he might find some reaction there. "I want the Austrians to know they have been punished. Reduce their western boundaries, liberate some of those disparate countries you were talking about, and secure a handsome payment for our treasury."

Talleyrand thought about all the little countries the Emperor wanted to "liberate" from the Austrian Empire, and how eagerly they would seize the chance to make war on one another, wars that would likely continue for hundreds of years. Was it part of the Emperor's plan to plunge that part of Europe into strife? No, the Emperor had no plan. He had only his destiny.

The Emperor's mouth twitched, almost as if it were laboring to deliver a smile. It stopped short of such a thing, but the corners of his eyes crinkled and his face had the playful look he used on those occasions when he kept an important ambassador or head of state waiting for him.

"If you will not do it, I will find someone who will," he said.

Talleyrand, who endeavored to accommodate the unexpected with aplomb, was nevertheless puzzled by the remark. "Why would I not do it, Your Majesty?"

The Emperor studied him, as if searching for his reaction. "With your beliefs, a man of principle would resign rather than follow my instructions."

Talleyrand was not offended. To take offense, he would have to be one who aspired to be a man of principle. Talleyrand had no such aspiration. The only men of principle he had known were people from whom it was prudent to protect himself. And he never cared to be a man against whom people needed protection.

"I have little need for principles," said Talleyrand. "Your Majesty has enough for both of us."

The Emperor shook his head indulgently, as if in marvel at the precocity of a child, although he was fifteen years Talleyrand's junior. "In eight years I have never been able to tell the difference between your flattery and your insults." He stuffed a forkful of chicken into his mouth, chewed a moment, and then spoke around it. "But I suppose it doesn't matter. When you are finished with them, the Austrians will doubtless feel the same way."

"I can do no more than my best," said Talleyrand.

"Are you sure you won't try this chicken?" said the Emperor. "It *is* delicious."

Talleyrand was glad the cook would not have to be deported. He knew the man. His foie gras was excellent.

Talleyrand went to the negotiating table at Pressburg and, as graciously as he knew how, stripped the Austrian monarchy of everything, including its dignity. By the time he concluded the treaty, the Emperor Francis lost three million subjects and one-sixth of the revenues of the House of Hapsburg. Francis further agreed to pay an indemnity of forty million francs to the French Empire.

It was both a punitive and a handsome settlement, and Talleyrand's sovereign was grateful. Back in Paris, he called the foreign minister to his office at the Tuileries.

Talleyrand found him at his enormous desk reading the treaty.

"I might have hoped for a larger indemnity." The Emperor spoke without looking up. "But I think you did well."

"Had we been any harsher," said Talleyrand, "we would have destroyed the House of Hapsburg entirely."

"Is the House of Hapsburg any particular use to anyone?" The Emperor looked up from the treaty.

In bleaker moments, Talleyrand thought the Emperor's destiny was to destroy rather than spread French civilization. "A skilled hunter preserves something from the kill, as a token of the achievement."

The Emperor said nothing and looked back at the treaty.

Talleyrand took this as evidence of agreement, for silence was the Emperor's way of accepting another's point without conceding his own.

"Your Majesty," he said.

The Emperor did not look up from the treaty, but Talleyrand detected the movement of an eyebrow.

"Your Majesty," he said, "there is another matter that needs imperial attention."

The Emperor looked up. "What is it?"

"Now that the Empire has no enemies in Europe proper, it would behoove Your Majesty to shore up our flanks, so to speak."

"What are you talking about?"

"An alliance with the Tsar," said Talleyrand.

"The Tsar is allied with the Austrians," said the Emperor. "Do you forget he was among those I defeated?"

"Who could forget Your Majesty's victory?"

"Is the Tsar now a threat to me?" said the Emperor.

"Hardly," said Talleyrand.

The Emperor went back to reading the treaty. "Why should I seek an alliance with him, then? Why should I not simply subdue him?"

"A Russian alliance, Your Majesty, would allow the Empire to isolate the English completely."

The Emperor looked up again.

Napoleon's destiny might have been to conquer every country within reach, but his deepest desire was to destroy England, or at least damage it.

"I will think about this." He looked back at the treaty, but did not seem to read it quite as intently as he had before.

"If Your Majesty needs me no longer— "

"Wait a moment." Without looking up, the Emperor pushed an envelope, wrapped with blue ribbons and bearing the imperial seals, across the surface of the enormous desk.

Talleyrand limped up to the desk to take the envelope.

The Emperor turned the page of the treaty and continued to read as he spoke. "I have appointed you prince of Benevento." Still without looking up, he turned the next page.

Benevento? He was being given a country?

Talleyrand took the envelope. "Your Majesty, I don't know what to say."

"Good," said the Emperor. "Then I will not have to worry over the meaning of it."

It was the closest he had ever come to making a joke.

The principality of Benevento was a small enclave in the Kingdom of Naples and had been a papal state until the Emperor redrew the map of Italy. It had 40,000 inhabitants and generated an income that was about a fifth of what Talleyrand realized from Valençay.

Reinhardt, who was well connected in the community of professional administrators, found Talleyrand an Alsatian named Louis de Beer who was willing to go to Benevento (which Talleyrand renamed Bénévent) and act as his deputy. Talleyrand was particular with de Beer's instructions.

"Your first duty," he said, "is to expel the papal troops. But you are acting as my proxy, and you should be polite about it."

"Yes, Your Highness," said de Beer.

It was the first time anyone had called him that since he was a child at Chalais. But he was not born to his Bénéventan rule, and the title made him uncomfortable. Perhaps others without birthright thought it appropriate to be addressed as royalty, but he did not like it.

"Do not call me Highness," said Talleyrand. "I am less than that, although I may well be better. At any rate, Monsieur will suffice."

"Very well, Monsieur," said de Beer.

"I require that all official acts be published in French as well as Italian," Talleyrand continued. "You should open schools, where instruction is to be given in French, and they are to be open to anyone of Bénéventan birth, without expense."

De Beer's eyebrows went up.

Talleyrand was not surprised at his deputy's dubiousness. No other country in Europe offered public education to its citizens without charge.

"I have asked the Imperial Exchequer to write a budget that will reduce Bénéventan taxes by a third, and I intend to see to it my subjects are exempted from conscription into the Grand Army." If French civilization was to be lost in France, sacrificed on the altar of Empire, perhaps it could be preserved for future generations in Bénévent. Let them survive the Emperor's wars, learn French, and prosper.

"You are most generous to them, Monsieur," said de Beer. "Will your subjects have the opportunity to see you and thank you?"

"I doubt that they will," said Talleyrand. "The work of the Foreign Ministry is very demanding."

He might have enjoyed going to Bénévent and playing at being a prince. But it had become increasingly apparent to him that if he left France, the Emperor would be completely without restraint. Who knew what he might do then? Invade Russia? Lay siege to Moscow? Such an idea was laughable, of course, but the Emperor, in the grip of his destiny, was likely to act like a madman.

🦁   🦁   🦁

The Foreign Ministry sat astride an endless stream of international incidents and negotiations. Every time the Emperor redrew a national boundary (which Talleyrand often suspected was his second most favorite occupation), it created an international incident that had to be managed and dissipated by the Foreign Ministry. And when the Emperor was not in Paris redrawing boundaries, he was in the field laying waste to those who would oppose his cartography.

After each new conquest, Talleyrand went to the Emperor and advised him to treat the vanquished with magnanimity.

"I don't understand you," said the Emperor. "Why do you keep telling me to be friends with countries I have conquered?"

"Friendship is conducive to peace, Your Majesty."

But the Emperor did not seem to comprehend the benefits of peace.

"Would you give up your fortune?" said Napoleon. "You are bound to lose money if I take this advice. They come to you with their gifts and their tips and their bribes because they fear me. If they thought me benevolent, they would have no need to curry favor with you."

"I never turn away gifts, Your Majesty," said Talleyrand. "But I would gladly trade them for a peaceful Europe."

"I will never understand you," said the Emperor.

And Talleyrand realized he could truthfully say the same. He may be able to know exactly how the Emperor would act in a situation, but he would never truly appreciate why the man behaved as he did. Surely he did not actually believe in this destiny of his. The most powerful nation in the world in the hands of a man animated by the conviction that he was something more than mortal? The idea was too frightening to contemplate.

But Talleyrand saw with some gratification that he was still able to influence the Emperor, for within two years after Pressburg Napoleon announced that he wanted to meet with the Tsar of Russia with an eye toward making an alliance.

Talleyrand had never met Tsar Alexander, but he knew him well, having read everything ever written about him and having interviewed many people who knew him. The picture that emerged was that of a man from a different era. The age of the enlightened despot could be said to have ended in 1789, when the French Revolution began, but Alexander I continued to embrace the principles of a liberal-minded, well-educated absolutist, wielding power for the benefit of his country. Such a man must, of course, be limited in what he could achieve in a country as backward as Russia, but the Tsar had doubled the number of Russian universities. He had even instituted laws against some of the more barbarous punishments the Russian nobility habitually visited on the serfs.

Knowing his sovereign's penchant for ceremony and stage work, Talleyrand arranged for the meeting between the two emperors to take place on a raft in the River Niemen. He planned that both entourages would arrive at the river bank simultaneously, so as not to imply any precedence on either side. But Napoleon, ever the show-man, insisted on arriving early, and then he advanced with a small guard of honor another half kilometer so he could intercept the Tsar. When Alexander's party arrived, they found the Emperor of the French standing in the center of the road, wearing the uniform of a colonel.

Tsar Alexander descended from his coach without ceremony. When the two men shook hands, a cheer went up from all assembled. At Napoleon's insistence, the two men walked back to the raft together, out of earshot of anyone else. He then insisted that the formal discussions between the emperors take place in private.

Talleyrand gave his sovereign the draft treaty he had prepared and watched with everyone else as the two emperors boarded the raft and signaled for the boatmen to pull it to the center of the river with their ropes. The two rulers talked all day, while their entourages milled about impatiently on the shore.

At mid-afternoon Napoleon signaled the boatmen, and their raft was towed to shore again. Everyone dispersed to enjoy whatever food and entertainment the locale had to offer. When Talleyrand arrived at his rooms in a nearby château, there was a message waiting for him saying that the duchesse de Courland had arrived and would find great pleasure in meeting him.

Never one to deny a lady pleasure of any kind, Talleyrand called on her straightaway. She turned out to be a gracious and refined widow whose departed husband had been the last ruler of Courland, a minor Prussian duchy. She had dreams of living in Paris and exercising some influence in the highest social circles. She was a handsome woman, and her conversation was stimulating.

She had the most beautiful violet-eyed daughter, a thirteen-year-old girl named Dorothée who clearly preferred her own company to that of her elders. Talleyrand was nearly mesmerized by her exquisite appearance, but he did not get to enjoy it very much, for she asked permission to be excused after only the briefest of pleasantries.

Talleyrand continued his conversation with the duchesse, who was not particularly witty but had the redeeming quality of obviously believing the prince de Bénévent was one of the most important people in the civilized world.

One of the servants entered and announced Tsar Alexander. The poor man had no sooner made the announcement than he was nearly bowled over by the Tsar himself, who was, apparently, walking on his heels.

Talleyrand struggled to his feet, but the Tsar stopped him with a command.

"Please remain seated," he said. "I believe you have been made to stand enough today."

Talleyrand had never encountered such a civilized monarch.

"Thank you, Your Majesty."

Talleyrand's own emperor was thirty-eight years old — rather young to be the most powerful man in the world, perhaps. But the foreign minister judged the Tsar to be eight or ten years younger than Napoleon.

"To what do we owe the pleasure of this visit, Your Majesty?" said the duchesse de Courland.

Talleyrand suspected she already knew and had, in fact, planned this meeting. But he said nothing.

"To be frank," said the Tsar, "I have come in hopes of meeting the prince de Bénévent."

The young Tsar sat down beside the foreign minister and the two of them talked about the weather, the local food, and the Tsar's reforms in Russia.

"I learned politics and philosophy from my grandmother, who raised me," said the Tsar. "She treasured the old ways. It was she who taught the rest of Europe the principles of enlightened despotism."

The Tsar's grandmother was, of course, Catherine the Great.

"I learned my most valuable lessons from my grandmother as well," said Talleyrand.

The Tsar looked off in the distance for a moment. "I still miss her."

The Tsar was an exceedingly refined man, but Talleyrand saw what appeared to be pain in the depths of his eyes when he mentioned his grandmother. It made him feel uncommonly close to the Tsar.

They talked through dinner and then talked the evening away. The duchesse de Courland finally said something about the rigors of travel.

"Oh, yes," said Talleyrand. "Please excuse me for intruding on your hospitality. You must be in need of rest. I should go now."

He thought the Tsar looked disappointed.

Apparently the duchesse saw the Tsar's look as well.

"If you could excuse me," she said, "I will retire. But I beg you to stay here and talk as long as you wish." She made a subtle gesture in the direction of the brandy bottle on the table, and suddenly the servant was at the Tsar's side, refilling his glass.

After the duchesse took her leave, the Tsar motioned for the servants to leave as well. He leaned toward Talleyrand and reached into the inside pocket of his coat.

He took out a folded sheaf of papers and handed them to Talleyrand. "I would like your advice on something."

Talleyrand took the papers. It was a draft treaty between the French Empire and the Russian Empire — one he had never seen before. It was written in Napoleon's own hand. He read it over. Its main provision was to bind Russia to a military alliance with France, particularly as regarded Austria. It specified that an Austrian attack on any territory under the protection of the French Empire, which was nearly any territory between the Rhine and Russia proper, would be considered an attack on Russia.

So Napoleon was planning an alliance of mutual protection with Russia that he did not want Talleyrand to know about, at least until it was accomplished. That could mean only one thing. He intended to attack some other country (Spain and Portugal were the only ones left that were not protected by a waterway), and wanted to make certain Austria would be secure.

Talleyrand looked up at the Tsar, who was looking away. Apparently, he knew that Talleyrand knew nothing of Napoleon's draft treaty and wanted to spare him embarrassment.

He looked back at the treaty and the Emperor's schoolboy penmanship. What was Talleyrand to do? If he collaborated with the Tsar, it would be treason. Were he found out, he would doubtless face a firing squad. But if this treaty were enacted, it would probably mean another war of conquest.

"My grandmother," the Tsar said quietly, "was one of the greatest Russians who ever lived, but what she was most proud of was being one of the great Europeans. She taught me that there is a distinction."

It was a distinction Talleyrand often made in his own mind. A Périgord, a Frenchman, a European, a civilized human being — the surest way to create conflict among one's various connections to the world was to introduce a barbarian like Napoleon into the landscape.

He found it interesting that Russia, the most uncivilized of European countries, had a civilized ruler, while France, the most civilized, had an uncivilized one.

"I would advise Your Majesty not to sign this," he said.

"Shall I risk war with the French Empire?" said the Tsar.

"The French people do not want war with Russia," said Talleyrand. "They do not, in fact, want war at all — although they may find themselves pushed willy-nilly into it. They may not know it, but right now they depend on Your Majesty and his greatness of spirit to protect them."

The Tsar nodded.

"Shall I provide Your Majesty with the draft of a new treaty that might be less restrictive to Your Majesty's interests?"

Thus did the negotiations continue. The Tsar and the Emperor talked each day, and each evening the Tsar met with Talleyrand in the apartments of the duchesse de Courland to discuss strategy. Talleyrand knew he was risking everything, and it was by no means certain his strategy for peace in Europe would prevail. But he knew the Emperor's plan (if plan it was) to wage constant war throughout Europe would never succeed, and it would only destroy him and his country with it.

By the time the negotiations were over, Napoleon and Alexander had divided Poland and Prussia and various other provinces between them, but they established no military alliance. They agreed to nothing more than a mutual understanding. Talleyrand had won two things of immediate value: the friendship of Tsar Alexander and the promise of an alliance by marriage with the family of the duchesse de Courland. Her daughter, Dorothée, was pledged to the prince's nephew, Edmond, in a marriage that was to take place two years hence. This last was very important, for Talleyrand had come to realize that if Edmond were to marry a French woman, the Emperor would decide who his wife would be.

But the prince thought the most important thing he had won was the postponement of a new war, since the Emperor would not start anything that might distract him as long as the Austrians, sullen and chafing under their last settlement with him, were not taken out of the way.

Back in Paris, the Emperor summoned Talleyrand to the Tuileries again. Talleyrand was wary but not resentful. That the Emperor had tried to deceive him in the Russian negotiations was no cause for bitterness. If anything, it added a measure of interest to his daily work. Playing mouse to the Emperor's cat was infinitely more entertaining than acting as his courier.

As usual, the Emperor did not invite him to sit down.

"I am going to Spain," he said.

"Your Majesty?"

"I have a report that Portugal is contemplating an alliance with England," said the Emperor.

"They have always had close ties in trade," said Talleyrand.

"It is a good time for me to renew our friendship with King Charles," said the Emperor, as if Talleyrand had not spoken. "Our alliance with Russia secures the eastern frontier, so if the English are to commit any aggression toward Spain, we can respond without fear of the Austrians."

Talleyrand knew what "renewing friendship" meant, and King Charles probably would not survive it.

"Your Majesty," said Talleyrand, "my reading of the Russian treaty is that it is not a military alliance."

"Nonsense," said the Emperor. "That's what 'mutual understanding' means."

Talleyrand let nothing show on his face, but he was stunned. He had succeeded in keeping the Emperor from getting the military alliance he wanted. But the Emperor could not recognize that he had come away from those negotiations empty handed. How does one play cat-and-mouse with a blind cat?

"This is not a particularly good season for travel," said Talleyrand.

"You're talking to the man who marched an army over the Alps to fight a battle," said the Emperor.

"Yes, of course," said Talleyrand.

At that moment, he knew he was no longer capable of influencing the Emperor, much less of controlling him.

"Your Majesty will forgive me," said Talleyrand, "if I do not accompany the imperial mission."

"Oh?" The Emperor looked questioning, but not particularly surprised.

Talleyrand had a sudden inspiration. "I have been thinking about this for some time," he said, "and I believe it is time to allow some of the Empire's younger men to begin to take on more responsibility. They must learn to exercise power in ministerial positions if this Empire is to outlive its founders."

The Emperor looked solemn, and Talleyrand knew the reasoning appealed to him. He fancied himself the architect of a permanent monument to that destiny of his.

"You are still a Vice-Grand Elector," said the Emperor.

"Of course, Your Majesty," said Talleyrand, "and I will continue to execute those duties as faithfully as I am able. But I would like to recommend my deputy, Reinhardt, as the foreign minister."

"A good man," said the Emperor. "So be it."

❧   ❧   ❧

The Emperor started toward the border in the spring.

Talleyrand wished the Emperor good speed and good fortune on his Spanish trip and then prepared to begin his retirement at Valençay. He thought briefly about a state visit to Bénévent, but at that moment rest seemed a great deal more important. And besides, the Emperor was certain to undertake some folly while he was in Spain, and Talleyrand did not want to be out of the country during an international crisis.

He told Catherine to pack for Valençay. She was plainly disappointed to be leaving Paris. But he pointed out to her that she should encounter a whole new group of people who would be pleased to meet a princess and address her as Serene Highness, a title she much preferred to Madame de Talleyrand. She showed a childlike delight at the prospect, but Talleyrand no longer enjoyed her delight the way he once had. She did not wear it as well since she had become heavy. She had not slept with him in years, but neither had he asked her.

The trip to Valençay was uneventful, and the estate was quiet, which suited Talleyrand, even if it gave Catherine cause for complaint. For a few weeks the prince de Bénévent was able to relax and catch up on his reading. An old friend, Adelaïde de Souza (whom he had once known as Adelaïde de Flahaut), had written a novel, and he was anxious to enjoy it, along with a number of literary papers and essays he had been collecting against the opportunity of reading them. He finished several of the essays, a book on natural history, and an undistinguished tract of English political economy before he sat down with Adelaïde's book a week after he had arrived. He read several chapters in the morning and then just before bestirring himself for a cup of coffee, one of the servants told him he had a visitor. It was Reinhardt.

Talleyrand met him in the reception hall near the front door.

"What brings you from Paris, my dear friend?"

"The need for advice and guidance," said Reinhardt. "I have a letter from the King of Spain." Reinhardt began removing a large sheaf of papers from the portfolio he was carrying. "It is a public declaration."

"Can you give me its essence?"

"King Charles," said Reinhardt, "has abdicated his throne in favor of his son Ferdinand. Ferdinand has abdicated in favor of Joseph Bonaparte."

It all sounded like comic opera. A king steps aside for his son, and his son steps aside for an interloper. And, once again, the inexhaustible House of Bonaparte assumes control of an ancient throne at the point of a French bayonet.

Joseph, the Emperor's older brother, would doubtless make an excellent monarch — he had already been King of Naples, where he had proved a good neighbor to Bénévent — but this was the first time the Emperor had removed a king worthy of the name. Until now, he had contented himself with the manipulation of duchies and principalities, but Spain was not Lombardy or Naples or Westphalia. It was a nation.

"With all due respect to King Joseph," said Reinhardt, "a Bonaparte on the Spanish throne could provoke the English."

"Indeed," said Talleyrand. "Before you return to Paris, prepare a memorandum for the Emperor to that effect."

Reinhardt's face paled.

"We will send it on my signature," said Talleyrand. "I hold no official brief with him, but I am still a Vice-Grand Elector and I believe he still respects my advice."

Next morning, Reinhardt gave Talleyrand a draft of the memorandum. The prince studied it, corrected several phrasings, and asked for a final copy, which he signed.

Reinhardt returned to Paris, saying he would put it in the next diplomatic pouch bound for Spain.

Talleyrand felt it was still his duty to give the Emperor the best advice of which he was capable, but he was glad he was no longer in the Emperor's service.

Talleyrand had no particular veneration for the Spanish monarchy, but he felt some responsibility for the making of the Emperor, and now he felt like the first officer on a ship whose captain was determined to run her aground. It was time to lower the boats and leave the man to his own devices.

Talleyrand decided to go back to Paris in a month and take the lay of the land. But he had more resting to do. He recommenced his reading and began entertaining some of the locals in the evening. He nearly managed to forget that Spain existed — until the morning one of the servants told him there was a troop of cavalry at the gate.

Talleyrand met the troop's commander in the reception room near the main door. The commander was a captain, a courteous-looking man and quite young, as might be expected in the Grand Army, where longevity was uncommon. He stood at rigid attention, cradling a crested helmet in his left arm.

The captain clicked his bootheels and handed the prince a letter. It bore the seal of the Emperor and was addressed to Charles-Maurice de Talleyrand-Périgord, prince de Bénévent. Talleyrand opened it and held it at arm's length for reading.

The letter said that Talleyrand was to receive visitors at Valençay — Ferdinand, the former King of Spain, his younger brother, and his uncle. It advised him to treat them decently but to receive them without ceremony. It said Talleyrand could expect to have these guests for a week to ten days, and during that time he should ascertain what they were thinking, the better to advise the

Emperor on what to do with them. It was signed   Napoleon, Emperor of the French.

Talleyrand looked from the letter to the young captain. It would be foolish to believe the young man did not
know something of its contents.

"Do you know when they are to arrive?" he said.

"We left them under the charge of Colonel Henri," said
the captain. "He is a superior officer of the Gendarmerie
d'Élite. They were to have started this morning several
hours behind us, but the roads are surprisingly hard, and
they may be closer than that."

The Emperor knew Talleyrand opposed the destruction
of the Spanish monarchy. He knew, in fact, that the
entire civilized world would oppose it. It was obviously his
design by imprisoning Ferdinand VII at Talleyrand's home
to give the world the impression that his foreign minister
was an accomplice in this ill-considered scheme. And so
the prince de Bénévent was to embark on a new career:
part jailer, part innkeeper, part eavesdropper. The
Emperor seemed to have an inexhaustible fund of meth-
ods for making people feel small.

As Talleyrand came to himself from his ruminations
and looked at the young captain before him, he could hear
the distant call of a coachman's trumpet, followed by the
rapid footsteps of several of his servants running down his
hallways.

FIFTEEN

"WE HAVE GUESTS arriving," Talleyrand said to his servant. "I want you to install them in the east wing."

"Shall I remove Your Highness's effects from his apartment?"

"Have my things taken to the west wing," said Talleyrand. "The east wing has a chapel, and I suspect our guests will want to use it more than I."

The servant departed to give the orders. Talleyrand looked out the third-floor window and saw a procession of ancient coaches arriving. They were of a type he had not seen since his youth, and they had been old then. One of them bore the coat of arms of the Spanish House of Bourbon — obviously King Ferdinand's coach.

The coaches were surrounded by mounted gendarmes. Two of the horsemen dismounted and started toward the main door of the mansion. Two other horsemen dismounted and went to open doors of the two least opulent coaches. The rest of the gendarmes remained mounted. Their horses seemed well behaved.

Well, if he were to act the part of innkeeper, he must do it politely. He started downstairs to receive the royal party properly at the main door.

In the foyer he encountered Colonel Henri, a brutish-looking officer of the gendarmerie. There were a half dozen people in strange, foreign dress standing well behind him, flanked by gendarmes. Colonel Henri's uniform was whitened with road dust and he appeared not to have bathed in a week.

"These are just part of the retinue." Colonel Henri gestured at the foreigners under guard. "The king and the princes are still out in the coaches." He handed Talleyrand a creased and soiled piece of paper. "I'll need a receipt for the prisoners, Monsieur."

"What prisoners are you referring to, Colonel?" said Talleyrand.

"The Spaniards."

"Surely you do not mean the Spanish royal family?" said Talleyrand.

"My orders are to deliver them and get a receipt," said the Colonel.

"I'll sign your receipt." Talleyrand took the paper and signaled to one of the servants for a pen. "And I will thank you to understand that you are escorting allies of the Empire, not criminals."

The servant brought the pen. Talleyrand took the receipt to the ornate sideboard that stood in the hallway. He bent over to sign it. "I hope they give a good account of your treatment of them."

He straightened and handed the signed receipt to his servant, who took it to Colonel Henri.

"It matters very little to me," said Colonel Henri. "I answer to the Emperor." He handed the receipt to an officer standing next to him. "If you will show me where the Spaniards are to be billeted, I will give instructions to their guards."

"Guards?"

"My orders are to keep them in the sight of my men at all times." He looked around the foyer, as if gauging its defensibility.

"Colonel, I must tell you that you are in Valençay. This estate is under the power and authority of a sovereign prince and a Vice-Grand Elector. The Emperor reigns in neither the corridors nor the grounds here. I will take responsibility for the princes. You are not needed here."

The Colonel said nothing, but stared at him with a surly expression.

"I am sure you and your men will be better employed back in Paris," said Talleyrand, "in pursuit of the enemies of France."

The Colonel did not move.

"None of which you will find here," added Talleyrand.

He thought he saw a weakening of the Colonel's expression.

"I will be sitting down directly to write to the Emperor about the safe arrival of the Empire's guests," said Talleyrand. "I will be sure to tell him how coopera-tive you have been."

That seemed to mollify the policeman, who turned and left, followed by the rest of his men, leaving the group of foreigners standing in the foyer, looking as if they did not quite comprehend what was happening.

Talleyrand could decide later whether it was worth writing a letter to Fouché, the Minister of Police, about the surly Colonel Henri. It would be a decision that re-quired thought, for Talleyrand did not know if his criti-cism was more likely to enhance or diminish Colonel Henri's fortunes in the police ministry. Talleyrand and Fouché were known throughout Paris as rivals, and the less reputable newspapers and gossips branded them enemies.

One of the foreigners, a man of courtly appearance, separated himself from the others and approached Talleyrand.

"Don José Miguel de Carvajal, Your Highness," said the man. "I am duc of San Carlos and attendant to the King. We are in your debt for your kindness."

"Valençay is at the King's disposal," said Talleyrand.

"Please tell him that I will not bother him with tedious introductions until he has had the opportunity to rest from his journey, and that I hope to see him at dinner this evening."

"May I say," said the duc of San Carlos, "that we have not been shown such courtesy since your emperor arrived in our country."

Talleyrand did not miss the indirect criticism of Napoleon. The duc was obviously well mannered, but there was clearly something about being marched around at bayonet-point that reduced one's self-restraint.

"We are all on holiday here," said Talleyrand. "Let us relax and enjoy it."

The duc of San Carlos looked dubious, but he and the rest of the party went back outside to the coaches, and Talleyrand started back upstairs.

There was a great deal to arrange before dinner that evening. He had to ask the cook if he had any experience with Spanish dishes. He had to send inquiries to find appropriately aged companions for the princes. He had to locate and engage a guitar player. So many details, negotiations, letters.

Entertaining the Spanish royal family promised to be only slightly less demanding than running the Ministry of Foreign Affairs. Was it worth the effort to make these young men comfortable? Well, it was always useful to make friends.

The Spanish princes were Bourbons, cousins to the self-styled Louis XVIII, who — from his residence in England — claimed to be the legitimate monarch of France. A man of self-indulgence and unparalleled density, Louis XVIII could not accept the world as it is and, lacking the power to change it, remedied the matter by changing his perception of it. Talleyrand had met the "king" only briefly, back in 1781, but it was long enough to see that

the man had a narrowness of view sufficient to give royalty a bad name.

But as boorish and stupid as the would-be French
king was, the Emperor Napoleon — in his apparent head-
long drive to self-destruction — might yet prove to be
Louis' strongest supporter in his desire to reclaim France.

Talleyrand found himself waiting for his guests at dinner. He did not mind, but Catherine complained.

"We are Serene Highnesses," she said. "Should they
not show some consideration?"

It occurred to Talleyrand that being royalty seemed to
require insensitivity to the feelings and concerns of those
around you. He had yet to meet anyone above the rank of
duc who had the imagination to put himself in another's
place. This was obviously not a hereditary characteristic,
for he had watched the Emperor Napoleon acquire it since
his coronation.

When the young king and his brothers, the princes,
finally arrived, Talleyrand could have recognized them
even if they had disguised themselves with sensitive
behavior, for they had the pale color, dark hair, and wide
eyes he had seen in portraits of the Spanish Bourbons.

Catherine's pique evaporated immediately.

"Your Majesty." Catherine curtseyed. "This is the
honor of a lifetime."

Ferdinand merely nodded and looked around the room.
He was wary of people, even servants. Talleyrand could
only imagine the trials this family had endured at the
hands of theEmperor.

The duc of San Carlos, however, compensated for
Ferdinand's lack of conversation.

"Your Highness." He took Catherine's hand, bowed,
and pressed his lips to her knuckles. "I am Don Jose
Miguel de Carvajal, duc of San Carlos and attendant to
the King. May I tell you what a pleasure it is to be in the
presence of a princess so refined."

"Oh," said Catherine, apparently forgetting she had been slighted by her guests' tardiness.

"And so beautiful," added the duc of San Carlos.

Catherine laughed, and her face took on an expression Talleyrand had rarely seen since the evening she had entertained his dinner guests nude.

Polite to a fault, the Spanish princes were nevertheless reserved and wary throughout dinner. It must be difficult for them to know what to make of being entertained by one of the three to four most powerful men in the French Empire.

Talleyrand did what he could to put them at ease, and he was pleased to see their expressions soften at the sound of guitar music. But by the end of the evening, the only people in the party who seemed at all relaxed were Catherine and the duc of San Carlos. They excused themselves during fruit and cheese to take a walk in the garden under the moonlight.

Talleyrand watched them leave the dining room. Catherine giggled fetchingly, and the duc was clearly enthralled by her. Well he might be. Her prodigious appetite had rounded her body in places it had once been flat, but she still carried herself with the grace of an antelope. The prince turned back to his royal guest.

"I hope Your Majesty will speak up if he should discover any inconveniences here at Valençay," said Talleyrand, "and tell us if there is anything we can do to make his stay more pleasant."

Ferdinand looked at him with a hardened jaw and a wounded expression in his eyes. "Thank you."

"We have an excellent library. Perhaps the princes would enjoy some reading." Talleyrand looked at the young men across the table.

"Reading?" said Antonio.

"Valençay has the largest collection outside Paris,"

said Talleyrand, "and there are current books in every major language."

"Books?" said Charles.

The princes seemed not to comprehend the benefits of reading, and Talleyrand thought that if he had harbored any doubts, this would convince him he was in the presence of Bourbons.

Over the next several days, Talleyrand found his charges to be an object of curiosity. His gate was besieged with visitors, and the estate surrounded by spectactors. Valençay's staff had a job keeping the crowds at bay. Within the precincts of the estate, Talleyrand arranged hunts, shooting expeditions, fencing instructions, and dances for the princes.

The Spanish royal family did not eschew reading completely, and when the servants brought in the newspapers, Ferdinand had his brothers take turns reading the news of Spain aloud. The French newspapers carried stories of the glorious victories of the French armies against those few remaining Spaniards who were not yet prepared to accept Joseph Bonaparte as their king. Napoleon had left Spain for Erfurt to conclude negotiations on continuing Austrian neutrality.

The princes seemed pleased at the resistance of their people, but King Ferdinand became thoughtful on hearing these stories.

On the eleventh day of the princes' visit, Talleyrand began to understand that the "week to ten days" he was promised for the visit should be interpreted liberally.

Spring turned into summer, and life proceeded uneventfully at Valençay. The princes pursued their recreation in whatever ways they could. Ferdinand brooded. Catherine took walks with the duc of San Carlos. Everyone but Talleyrand attended mass at least twice a day.

Two weeks after Bastille Day, Reinhardt arrived from Paris. Talleyrand was glad to see him.

"I thought these might be of some use to you." Reinhardt opened a valise filled with English newspapers.

What Talleyrand read in the foreign newspapers did not shock him (nothing shocked him), but it gave him a completely different picture of Spanish affairs than what he had from the French newspapers.

According to the English accounts, after the princes had been taken out of Spain, the population rose against the French troops. A coterie of Spaniards had formed a provisional government that called on all Spaniards to resist French tyranny and demanded the return of King Ferdinand, whom they called *el deseado*. The Desired. Talleyrand thought about the sullen, brooding man in the east wing of his château and marveled at the Spanish imagination.

The French troops had been driven out of Madrid and King Joseph ousted from the seat of his government. A corps of 23,000 French soldiers had capitulated in Bailén. Everywhere, French units were harried by guerilla fighting.

How strange politics could be!

Napoleon was not a man of keen judgment, but Talleyrand knew the constitution he had given Spain enlarged the rights of Spaniards far beyond anything they had known before. It provided them with many of the benefits of the Code Napoléon, and Joseph Bonaparte was a perceptive and liberal statesman, and Spain's first constitutional monarch.

But the Spaniards reacted to these innovations in the same way the princes had reacted to Talleyrand's offer of his library. They turned them down.

"The military situation is grave," said Reinhardt. "This is no riot or jacquerie. The Emperor has left Erfurt early because the Austrians now refuse to negotiate. Seeing he will be occupied in Spain, they have begun to mobilize for war. The Emperor is now on his way to Spain with 300,000 troops."

Reinhardt was right. There was no precedent in history for the rising of an entire nation. "How is Paris taking the news?"

"Paris has no news to speak of," said Reinhardt. "All public reports are censored by Fouché. The city remains ignorant of the Emperor's misfortunes. It is just as well. If news of the reversals got out, it would cause panic in the streets and on the stock exchange."

Talleyrand understood it was time to go to Paris and see his broker.

"I shall go with you when you return to ‘ Paris," he said.

There were not many preparations to make. He wanted to say au revoir to Ferdinand, so he asked a servant to fetch the duc of San Carlos. Talleyrand knew exactly where the duc was, but he thought it would be awkward to go to Catherine's bedroom himself.

The duc finally turned up (not noticeably in dishabille) and hastily arranged a meeting between his king and their host. Ferdinand received the prince in Talleyrand's own favorite sitting room.

"I am pleased you have come, my friend," said Ferdinand. "I wanted your advice on a matter of some consequence."

"I am at your service, Your Majesty," said Talleyrand.

Ferdinand handed Talleyrand a letter. "This is the draft of a letter I have prepared for the Emperor. I have not yet applied my seal, and I hope you will read it and give me your best advice." Ferdinand gestured for Talleyrand to sit down.

Talleyrand took the letter and sat down with it.

It was one of the most remarkable things he had ever read in his life. It addressed Napoleon as "cousin," just as

if the Emperor was a man of royal blood. It congratulated
him in the most effusive terms on the glorious victories
Ferdinand had been reading about in the French newspapers. And it begged for the hand of a Bonaparte woman
in marriage.

"I wish the Emperor to know that I accept him as an
equal," said Ferdinand, "and that I acknowledge the power
of his position. I intend ultimately to request the grant of
a fiefdom commensurate with my status."

Talleyrand had not heard the word fiefdom in decades,
and it occurred to him that Ferdinand was living in a different century. He knew that the Emperor would not react
to this letter the way Ferdinand hoped. It was even an
open question now whether the Emperor could maintain
his hold on Ferdinand's country. The Spaniards may yet
force him to return *el deseado*.

He could say none of these things to the King.
Talleyrand was, after all, a citizen of the Empire.

"Your Majesty," he said, "perhaps it is not a propitious
time to be writing to the Emperor. He will likely visit
Valençay some time before next winter, and Your Majesty
could speak with him personally."

"Nonsense," said Ferdinand. "There's no time to waste
in these matters. I must begin strengthening the bonds of
friendship with him immediately."

They continued to talk about it for a few minutes, but
there was nothing Talleyrand could say to dissuade
Ferdinand from his course of action.

In the end, Talleyrand gave up his resistance to the
letter. It simply did not seem as pressing as the need to
get to Paris and see his broker.

Sixteen

IT WAS GOOD TO BE BACK in Paris, even if the city was edgy and beset with rumors of French military reversals.

Talleyrand's first order of business was to see his broker. He told the broker he wished him to go to the Bourse and sell contracts for the delivery of various shares — none of which he owned — two months hence. The broker arranged the contracts at the current share prices, so that if the prices went down before he delivered them, Talleyrand would buy them at the new, lower price and deliver them at the contracted price. Any decline in share value was thus translated into gain. Talleyrand's broker was experienced in these arrangements, which was one of the reasons Talleyrand used the man. One with insight into the future must create strategies for profiting by falling share prices as well as rising ones.

Talleyrand stood to lose in the event of a general increase in share prices, but he felt that was unlikely as more and more of the world came to recognize that France was ruled by a madman.

Talleyrand's judgment in the Bourse was well respected, and his broker was likely to sell such contracts on his own behalf as well as Talleyrand's. The effect of these contract sales would be felt in the Bourse immediately. Speculators less experienced than Talley rand were easily frightened, so many would join the movement early. With any luck, it could create stampede and perhaps

panic, which would handsomely reward the earliest contract sellers.

The Emperor was laying waste to Spain and imposing
houseguests on people in the most uncivilized manner, but
perhaps he could be the engine of prosperity for those
whom he used so rudely.

Next, Talleyrand sought a meeting with Fouché, the
Minister of Police. He had known Fouché since the days
of the National Assembly. They both lost clerical robes in
the early days of the Revolution. But Talleyrand was
abroad for the rise and fall of the Republic of Virtue.
Fouché was too much a man of principle to leave the
country to its own devices and had remained in France for
those two years, avoiding execution chiefly — Talleyrand
had been given to understand — by a program of aggres-
sive denunciations.

Denunciation seemed to suit him, and he apparently
decided it was his calling. Although Fouché had been
somewhat out of favor under the Directoire, General
Bonaparte recognized a talent in the man and elevated
him rapidly under the Consulate.

Whatever else the Consulate had brought to France
after the Directoire, it also brought an increase in "spon-
taneous" massacres, mysterious disappearances, timely
suicides, and bombings. Talleyrand knew Fouché was
behind most of these incidents. The man was a genius,
really. The more bombings and massacres, the more the
public demanded the protection of the police, and the
more powerful Fouché became. Consul Bonaparte, whom
the public saw as a source of protection from the violence,
was granted more and more power to deal with it.

Ultimately, Consul Bonaparte became Emperor
Napoleon I with the blessings of the Senate, and the principles of liberty and fraternity were thus saved.

In 1804, the country had been beset with royalist

plots, most of which Talleyrand thought were figments of the Emperor's imagination, incited by intelligence provided by his Minister of Police. No royalist plotters were found that year, although it was said the duc d'Enghien, a foreigner, was the focal point of a conspiracy. Talleyrand tried to point out to the Emperor that the duc was harmless as long as he did not come to France, but after the coronation the Emperor rarely listened to his foreign minister's advice.

When the Emperor told Talleyrand he was going to send Fouché after the duc d'Enghien, Talleyrand decided to enjoy the comic opera aspect of the mission and said nothing. He wished later he had done something to stop it, for the comic opera ended a week later when it was learned Fouché had crossed the Rhine with a small band of men, kidnapped the duc from his lover's home in Baden, brought him back to France, and had him shot by firing squad.

Talleyrand did little to strengthen his friendship with Fouché after that. He treated him with the utmost respect (that a man is a murderer is no excuse to be impolite to him), but he simply did not seek his company.

"To what do I owe the honor of this visit, Prince?" Fouché stood up from his desk and offered his hand.

The prince looked at the hand for a moment before grasping it. Fouché was cleaner under the fingernails than any man in Paris.

Fouché gestured toward a chair across from his desk.

Talleyrand sat. "You may be aware that the princes of the Spanish House of Bourbon are living at Valençay."

"Yes, of course," said Fouché. "It was my idea."

Hearing that, Talleyrand was glad the princes had arrived alive. "It was a good one."

"I hope it hasn't inconvenienced you," said Fouché.

"Not the princes themselves," said Talleyrand. "They are very pleasant people. But they have occasioned a great deal of local curiosity, and Valençay is beset with spectators. I wanted to ask if you thought you could assign a small detachment of gendarmes to the estate to help control the crowds."

"You had the opportunity to have Colonel Henri and his men there," said Fouché, "but you sent them away."

"I did not think it appropriate to have the princes under guard," said Talleyrand. "I just want someone there now to help control those who come to look at them."

"Yes, I see." Fouché thought for a moment. "You shall have your gendarmes."

"Thank you," said Talleyrand.

"Tell me," said the Minister of Police, "why have you not spoken to me since the incident of the foreign duc? Have you been avoiding me? Did I not carry out your plan correctly?"

"My plan?"

"The Emperor said it was your plan to return the duc to France for interrogation."

"I am afraid it was the Emperor's plan alone," said Talleyrand. "I had nothing to do with it except in my failure to attempt dissuading the Emperor from it."

"It seemed like a plan of yours." Fouché seemed put out, as if he thought he'd been deceived by the Emperor.

Talleyrand realized that Fouché regretted the death of d'Enghien. He wondered if he might use this to his advantage. "I assure you," he said, choosing his words carefully, "that I don't make plans that may ultimately appear to the world to be crimes."

Fouché was silent for some moments. "It was worse than a crime," he said at last. "It was a mistake."

🦁　　🦁　　🦁

Talleyrand stayed on in Paris for some weeks. He saw
Fouché a number of times, and he learned that the
French military situation was at least as bad as the
English newspapers had portrayed it to be. It was part of
Fouché's responsibilities to make certain the public re-
mained ignorant of the full extent of the casualty lists.

"The Emperor has reduced the Spanish army to scat-
tered gangs," he said, "but when he annihilates one of
these gangs, the civilians themselves fight — from house
to house. And now the British have invaded from
Portugal. The situation does not look good at all."

"When the governing council next meets," said
Talleyrand, "I will say publicly what I say to you here,
that the Spanish undertaking is ill-advised and should be
stopped before it ruins France as it has the Emperor's
brother."

The problem grew worse. It seemed that no matter
how many the French troops killed, the Spaniards could
not be persuaded of their role in realizing the Emperor's
destiny. The more reverses the French had in the field,
the more restive the Empire's allies and satellites became.
Austria took to the field against Napoleon.

In a Paris salon one evening, the conversation came
around to Spain. Talleyrand observed that France might
be better off if the Emperor would leave the Spaniards to
their own devices and return home to stabilize the stock
exchange. He knew his remarks would get back to the
Emperor, and he hoped they would gain his attention
more readily than any letter he might write him directly.
Fouché was there, nodding his encouragement.

Talleyrand found himself in the strange position of
being in agreement with the policeman. He decided to invite him to his next reception. He began to encounter him
more and more often in various Paris salons, and he wondered what intelligence Fouché had brought to bear on

various hostesses that would get him invited, for he had not been a regular figure in Paris society.

Talleyrand was at home in the house on rue St. Florentin, giving Auguste orders regarding his packing for the return to Valençay, when the maid came in to tell him there was a woman in the drawing room to see him.

"Who is it?"

"She would not give her name, Monsieur."

One of the hazards of being influential is strangers asking for favors. But Talleyrand hated to send anyone away without first hearing what she wanted from him.

He went to the drawing room.

When he entered the room, his guest stood up and smiled at him. Had he been studying a painting of this woman, he might not have known her. But standing in the same room with her, he felt her presence in almost the same way he had thirty years before. It was Angelique.

Time had been good to her appearance. She was an extremely handsome woman in her fifties, and it occurred to him that this may well be a woman's best age, at least from a man's point of view.

"Hello, Aumônier," she said.

He embraced her, and for the second time in his life he was at a loss for words. He remembered that the first time was in her presence as well. His mind boiled with questions, none of which it would have been polite to ask.

"How are you?" he said at last.

"I have been well," she said. "I have returned to France only recently."

"I understood you went to America after the death of Monsieur Boucher."

"No," she said. "I went to England with my little boys."

"But I was in England, too," said Talleyrand, as if noting they had stayed at the same hotel one weekend.

"It is not large," said Angelique, "but it is a whole country, after all."

"Did you go on the stage?"

"No," she said. "I married. I am the comtesse de Villèle. We have only just returned to France under the Emperor's amnesty."

The two sat and chatted for most of the rest of the day. Talleyrand was delighted that her wit remained sharp and playful as ever. He thought she must have been the delight of the expatriate community in England.

Toward the end of the afternoon, the conversation worked around to the topic that Angelique had apparently come to pursue.

"Both of my sons want to go to Spain and fight for the Emperor." Her voice was sad, and it was clear she opposed her sons' desires.

"I am sorry," said the prince.

"Oh, but I am certain it is not your fault, Aumônier," she said.

"You are right. It is not," he said. "But I was expressing sympathy rather than regret."

"I understand that you have opposed the Spanish war from the beginning," she said.

"That's true."

"You and Monsieur Fouché are the talk of my social circle," she said. "Among the older nobility, there is much speculation as to whether two old enemies have taken common cause against the Emperor to stop this campaign."

"I am afraid the talk in your circle is ill-informed," said the prince. "I am not foolish enough to oppose the Emperor in anything other than matters of opinion. Besides, Fouché was never my enemy. I like to think I have no enemies."

"I am certain you do not." She smiled.

For a moment, Talleyrand wondered how she would react if he attempted to seduce her. But the moment passed, for he found it much easier these days to control his desires, and she seemed to prefer talking politics.

"The Emperor has enemies," she said. "They are massed on the borders. The comte d'Artois, brother of Louis XVIII, is attempting to raise troops."

"The comte d'Artois," said Talleyrand. "He and I had a long conversation in 1789, the night he left France with the other royals."

Angelique looked around the room, as if to ascertain that no one was listening. "You could be in touch with him if you want to be," she said. "I know a man, the baron de Vitrolles, who would carry a message on your behalf."

"No, thank you," said Talleyrand.

They chatted for a while longer, and then she took her leave. Talleyrand saw her to the door, then he watched out the window as she climbed into her carriage, which was very smart and harnessed to four well-groomed horses. She had not come to see him out of affection but to assess his sympathies to the royalists. She was the best candidate the royalists could possibly send. Even after thirty years, she knew he would not report a word of the conversation to anyone, lest she be implicated.

He was not resentful, for he had seen affection as well as mission in her eyes. He himself had never subscribed to the growing fashion of making distinctions among business, personal, and pleasurable matters. To him they were all parts of life. If their situations had been reversed, he would be doing the same.

He wondered if he would see her again. But he knew it would not be this week, for the city was becoming too nervous, and he wanted to return to Valençay.

⁂

At Valençay he found Fouché's gendarmes in place, controlling the crowds of people who surrounded the château. Inside the grounds, however, it was peaceful. He sent word to his guests and to Catherine that he would see them at dinner that night, then he retreated to his study to read the correspondence that had come for him in his absence. Most of it was quite routine, but there was a short letter from the Emperor. It was two sentences long.

> *Prince Ferdinand, in writing to me,*
> *addresses me as his cousin. Try to have the*
> *duc of San Carlos understand that this is*
> *ridiculous, and that he must simply call me*
> *Sire.*

At dinner that evening, prince Charles and prince Antonio were both delighted to see him. Prince Antonio had been taking lessons from the guitar player and wanted to play for him.

The duc of San Carlos seemed in excellent health, and Catherine actually seemed to glow. Talleyrand was pleased to see her so happy. Ferdinand, as usual, was reserved and aloof. He spoke only briefly.

"I have had no reply from the Emperor yet," he said. "But I expect some word before winter arrives."

"He must be very busy," said Talleyrand, omitting that what the Emperor was busy with was laying waste to his guest's country.

Two weeks later, he received word from Reinhardt that the Emperor was on his way to Paris from Spain and required Talleyrand for an emergency meeting of the council at the Tuileries.

So Talleyrand returned to Paris. He timed his trip so he would arrive before the Emperor. When he entered the Tuileries, the other council members — Cambacérès,

Lebrun, Decrès, and Fouché — were already there. So, unfortunately, was the Emperor. He was pacing the room, and when Talleyrand entered Napoleon turned to glower. "You're late," he said.

His face was pale and lacked the bloom the frightful David always gave him in the paintings. But Talleyrand knew that bloom had no more authenticity than the Emperor's field dispatches. From the first day he had known him, Napoleon's complexion was quite pallid, almost as if he were consumptive. The Emperor fixed him with his famous stare, the one Talleyrand had come to think of as the Stare ofIndomitable Destiny.

"I have arrived here from my Spanish headquarters in five days." He stopped pacing and gazed at Talleyrand. He wore the same look — Talleyrand had seen it before — of a man who believes another man has slept with his wife. When he spoke, his voice grated with restrained anger. "I crossed a mountain range and made my own roads through the snow. All you had to do was take a coach from Valençay."

The Emperor had not invited anyone to sit down and he himself seemed in no mood to sit. He paced so furiously that his military cloak, which was still spattered with the mud of his trip, actually fell from his shoulders. He stopped and stared at the cloak as he had stared at Talleyrand moments before. Then he walked over it, as if to punish it.

Talleyrand knew that the Emperor habitually treated inanimate objects — anything from a dinner plate to his hat — as enemies. In his experience, such objects care very little about the opinions of animate creatures, but the Emperor had taken his advice on this point no more readily than he would listen to Talleyrand's ideas about friendship among nations.

Talleyrand took advantage of the Emperor's distraction

with the fractious cloak to make his way to the other side
of the room, where there was a mantle he could lean
against.

The rest of the council members stood on one side of
the room and Talleyrand on the other. The Emperor paced
up and down the room between them with his hands
clasped behind his back.

"Bah," he said to his cloak. He walked to the end of
the room. He did not look up, but began to talk as he
stared at the floor, turned about, and marched to the
other end of the room.

"In my absence," he said, "the legislature had the
temerity to vote down provisions of the Code Napoléon
which I had submitted for their approval. Speculators
have attacked the Stock Exchange and brought it to the
brink of ruin." He looked up at Talleyrand. "Ministers of
my government meet without my permission or knowl-
edge."

The prince suspected the rest of this meeting might
not go well for him.

"Why should the legislature defy me and the speculators attack my Stock Exchange?" The Emperor looked
back down and began pacing again. "Could it be because
they expected the Spanish war would destroy me? Could
it be that the ministers of my government — my own
government — plan for my downfall?"

Talleyrand could see he was working himself into a
passion, and he decided to try to cool him down.

"Your Majesty — "

"Do not speak," he said. He looked at Talleyrand, then
turned his pacing toward him. "I have not made you a
prince of my empire that you should speak in my presence without leave. When I make a man a great
dignitary, he ceases to be free in word or thought and
becomes an instrument of my will."

He stopped about six feet short of Talleyrand, who

could see the other council members were watching him
with the fearful curiosity of spectators at an execution.
Talleyrand had never seen the Emperor look so forbid-
ding, and he realized he must cajole him out of his
bizarre mood or someone might be hurt.

"Your Majesty— "

"Do not speak!" he screamed. "You are unworthy to
speak in my presence! You are unworthy of the dignity
with which I have invested you. You are a thief! You have
failed in your duties, and you have deceived and betrayed
everyone. You hold nothing sacred. You do not believe in
God, and you would sell your family. I have given you
untold riches, and you repay me by denunciation. You
took it into your head that my affairs were going badly in
Spain, and you have had the gall to tell everyone that you
always opposed the Spanish campaign! This when you
were the one who originally suggested I go there and
would not let the matter rest until I had done so!"

Talleyrand did not laugh, although the idea that
anyone could influence the Emperor to do anything was
really quite amusing. All his ministers were, after all,
instruments of his will. But Napoleon looked at Talleyrand with the same gaze he must have trained on the city
walls when his artillery drove the British out of Lyons.

"And that wretched d'Enghien," he said. "Who was it
who told me he was in Baden? Who urged me constantly
to put him away?"

Talleyrand could see Fouché, the duc d'Enghien's
murderer, standing not twelve feet away.

"So what are you going to do now?" The Emperor took
several steps closer to Talleyrand. "What are your plans?"
He closed the remaining distance until there were mere
inches between their faces. The Emperor was several
inches shorter than his foreign minister, and Talleyrand
looked down on the frightful eyes and sneering mouth,

keeping his face as impassive as he could. This seemed to goad the Emperor further. He reached up and took hold of Talleyrand's chin between his thumb and forefinger. "What you deserve is to be smashed like glass. I cannot understand why I have never had you hanged from the gates of the Tuileries. I can do it. I can do it with a single word. I do not even need a word. I can do it with a gesture."

It occurred to Talleyrand that the Emperor was right. He could do it. Who would stop him? Fouché? Time slowed as the older man gazed down into the opaque, murderous eyes of his Emperor. Talleyrand could hear his own heartbeat, and he thought Napoleon must hear it as well, but the Emperor gave no sign.

"Bah." He released Talleyrand's chin. "I am engaged by my destiny. You're not worth it. You're nothing but shit in a silk stocking."

And then he stalked out of the room. Talleyrand could see the other council members were agitated, and he understood that any of them, Fouché in particular, was capable of taking him out and shooting him if he thought the Emperor really wanted it done. He had to pour oil on the waters.

"It's such a pity, gentlemen." He looked down at the cloak on the floor with the Emperor's bootprints all over it. "Such a great man. Such poor manners."

Fouché smiled knowingly, and several of the others nodded. They seemed to assume, as the prince had hoped they would, that the Emperor had been seized by a tantrum and would be over it briefly and restore Talleyrand to his good graces directly.

Talleyrand decided to remain in Paris for several weeks. He knew there were rumors all over the city, and if he were to return to Valençay it would give credence to the one that he had lost all influence in the government.

And, at this moment, he needed influence in the government, or at least the appearance of influence.

He was not surprised when Angelique came to see him two days after the Emperor's tantrum.

"How delightful to see you," said the prince.

Angelique smiled her radiant smile. "It is always a pleasure to be in your company, Aumônier."

"The last time we spoke," said Talleyrand, "you mentioned a friend of yours by the name of baron de Vitrolles."

"Yes?"

"I should like very much to meet him."

❋   ❋   ❋

It took the Emperor another six years to complete the process of self-destruction, something that he only managed after he had destroyed the cream of French manhood, much of it in the trackless wastes of Russian winter. As soon as the Spanish had taught Europe that he was not invincible, his alliances crumbled and his vanquished enemies stood against him once again.

The Emperor was a brilliant strategist in military matters, if not political ones. He fought his enemies to a standstill all over Europe, but even a man of destiny could not hold out against the combined military strength of the whole of Europe, particularly when his brutal behavior unified them in a common cause against him.

Bénévent, while nominally French, was able to maintain a de facto neutrality.

By spring of 1814, allied armies had crossed the border into France. The Emperor took himself to the countryside to personally raise troops to meet the new threat.

Talleyrand learned that Tsar Alexander was within two days' march of Paris. Still a Vice-Grand Elector of the

Empire and a member of the Regency Council, he went to the Empress and told her that he had received orders from the Emperor to evacuate the royal family. She and the Emperor's young son and the rest of the Regency Council fled the city.

The citizens of Paris, learning how close the allied armies were and seeing the imperial family depart, assumed the Empire was lost. The Parisians were not Spaniards. French civilization reasserted its spirit in the city. Its people refused to fight house to house but chose to repair to their drawing rooms and close their shutters.

Talleyrand sent his friend, the baron de Vitrolles, with a message to the comte d'Artois assuring him that there was a substantial faction in Paris that supported the return of the Bourbons. Then he sent a courier to Tsar Alexander with a message inviting him to enter Paris with his troops, where — the note said — he would be received with gracious hospitality at the home of the head of the provisional government of France, Charles-Maurice de Talleyrand-Périgord, prince de Bénévent.

SEVENTEEN

STRANGE HOW some of us can direct the fate of whole continents while others run after coaches seeking handouts, and in the end we all come to the same thing. Each of us must ultimately look into a bottomless abyss that fills his vision. And no matter how many people you have around you, you must look into it alone.

Father Dupanloup has taken it into his head that I cannot remember what is in the recantation and that is perhaps why I have so far refused to sign it. So he reads it aloud to the assembled company.

I listen to his voice droning the ritual phrases and sacred formulas. They are like wallpaper in a familiar room and do not separate themselves into anything noticeable or comprehensible. But from this wallpaper my sins emerge like lamp sconces.

". . . that I offended chastity and violated my sacred vows by living with a woman as if she were a wife . . . "

I would never have renounced you while you were alive, Catherine. But now you are beyond the reach of their disrespect and have no feelings to tread on. I will be your friend until my final breath.

". . . that I stole property from God's Holy Church on behalf of the late revolutionary government . . . "

I have stolen so much from so many in the course of my life, but now I disown the one "theft" I did with noble intent, the one that financed the Revolution and our high-minded ideals of liberty, equality, and fraternity.

". . . that I defrauded the apostolic succession established by God in performing a ceremony of ordination for the so-called constitutional bishops . . . "

I wonder what has become of my constitutional bishops. I wonder if any of them survived Fouché's dechristianization campaigns in the Terror.

". . . for these crimes and sins, I repent and beg the forgiveness of God . . . "

They sound like the least of my sins.

It is as if I apologize not for the things I have done, but for the Church's pettiness in being offended by them. I hope Father Dupanloup and the monsignor, who have been so understanding and so helpful, suffer no embarrassment when this document is spurned by the Pope. Perhaps they will see then that I knew what would happen, and they will feel badly used by me. But I will be in the ground then and will not care about their opinions.

I gaze about me, and I see my three attendants watching over me anxiously. I close my eyes to shut out their beseeching faces. Each has taken a turn asking me to sign the paper. Who will ask next?

I open my eyes again and look from face to face. Father Dupanloup. Pauline. Dorothée. The duchesse de Mortemart.

The duchesse. My duchesse.

It must be another of death's tricks — the person I most love conjured before my eyes. I have not seen her in eighty years, yet she has not changed a whit since the day I left her house at Chalais.

"It is time, Your Majesty," she says.

The others do not hear, and I realize I am the only one who knows she is there.

She bends down and touches my forehead. Her hand is warm and dry.

"May God heal you," she says. "The duchesse touches you."

I am overcome. I cannot speak.

"Your Majesty should finish it now," says the duchesse.

Is it that late? Is it time for me to take my winnings and depart?

"You will not win this, Your Majesty," says the duchesse. "It is not a game. It is a journey, a journey that is finished when you have done what you must."

What is it I must do?

"To sign their paper is the polite thing to do."

Of course. I have been so attentive to my game that I have forgotten the one thing that has always given me comfort in difficult times: my manners. My final act should not be to outwit the living but to put them at ease. Dying is no excuse for rudeness.

"Thank you, Duchesse."

I feel a hand against my face again. I look, and it is Dorothée. My other duchesse.

Pauline is weeping and has fallen to her knees by the bed. Father Dupanloup stands at the ready with his vestments and his oil.

They are such earnest people, living in the depths of their principles, their faith, their understanding.

"Might I trouble you to bring me the document," I say. "I will sign now."